Secrets

of the

PORCH

SUE ANN SELLON

TATE PUBLISHING
AND ENTERPRISES, LLC

Published by Tate Publishing & Enterprises, LLC
127 E. Trade Center Terrace | Mustang, Oklahoma 73064 USA
1.888.361.9473 | www.tatepublishing.com

Tate Publishing is committed to excellence in the publishing industry. The company reflects the philosophy established by the founders, based on Psalm 68:11,
"The Lord gave the word and great was the company of those who published it."

Book design copyright © 2014 by Tate Publishing, LLC. All rights reserved.
Cover design by Jan Sunday Quilaquil
Interior design by Jomel Pepito

Published in the United States of America

ISBN: 978-1-62994-545-3
1. Fiction / Romance / Suspense
2. Fiction / Romance / General
13.12.03

Dedication

I dedicate this book to my friend, my angel, my mom—a woman of incredible beauty, strength, and perseverance. Her love lies deep within me, and her soul touches my heart with grace. We are mirrors of each other. Everything I know, everything that I am, that which I will forever be, is because of her.

I also dedicate this book to my husband and best friend, Paul. Upon the beautiful red rocks of Sedona, Arizona, I dreamed of you. Our souls had been searching for one another, and only God knew how we longed for each other. I am overwhelmed and in awe of the beauty of your love. God created you for me and me for you. Your kindness and undying love have touched me in ways that I have never known before. This book and its messages wouldn't be possible without the truthfulness of love that you have brought me.

I have truly been blessed.

Finally, I dedicate this book to God for his faith in me and for allowing the truth to flow.

Acknowledgments

As I wake each morning, I am driven by the thoughts that stream down from the rays of sunlight. When I hear the birds singing outside the window, I am certain that I am in this time and this place because I have been led here, and my heart is free with his love. He moves me, and without his love and guidance, nothing could be as joyous and certain as the sunlight he shines through me.

Thank you, God.

Although the wings of those listed below aren't visible, they fly. They soar gracefully around me, leading me, carrying me. By their grace and wisdom, they are the inspiration that has sustained me in this life.

My husband, Dr. Paul D. Sellon
My father and mother, DeWayne and Darlene Nesiba
My father-in-law and mother-in-law, Robert and Virginia Sellon
My grandfather and grandmother, Hilda and Louis Nesiba
My sons, Christopher, Jonathon, and Alexander
My daughter, Carly
My grandchildren, Kylee, Alexis, Carter, Trevor, Ashton, and Paxton

My guides and angels:
Ms. Debbie Olis
Ms. Lee Calvin
Mrs. Ruth Heng
Mr. Charles Harter
Mr. Joseph Gerard

Introduction

Glancing at the old house that once stood strong, I laugh to myself as I reflect on memories past. I walk up the steps of the old weathered porch and notice the path worn into the wood, showing the scars of the many footsteps that have traveled across it: the little feet of children, the work boots of farmers, the heels of dressed-up ladies. Most of all, I recall quiet evenings of barefoot teas when I would sit alone with my thoughts. The flowerpots that once laced the stairs with a melody of colors are now empty and cracked. The swing is intact and moving gently back and forth. The fall breeze and leaves make their home on the porch as if they own it.

I look across the yard and see the silver maple standing tall and wide, displaying its leaves of golden yellow and orange, so bright that it looks as if God is among them. The garden I once tended so graciously with love is overgrown with weeds, as if it had barely existed. I can still hear the crackling sound of the old rockers where we would rest our tired bodies after a long day's work in the sun. I can feel the sweat dripping from my glass and running down my arm while I sip away on freshly squeezed lemonade. The memories are as clear in my mind as if it were only yesterday.

My transformation began here on this farm with love, love as powerful as a mighty storm but as subtle as a feather blowing in the wind. Influenced by that love, I began to change with each season.

Standing quietly on the porch, I remain frozen. The thought of returning here is as painful as the memory it holds. I see the old screen door and hesitate long before entering. Even though I sense the house inviting me inside, I only want to stand here.

I can hardly believe the first time I walked up these steps as a young girl, broken and consumed with fear beyond imagination. I was sixteen years old going on thirty, and Lila was sixty, believing in sixteen. My past followed me, and trouble presented itself wherever I went, or quite possibly, I presented trouble. I believed that I would always be a caterpillar. Lila saw the butterfly. A silent and unforeseen metamorphosis occurred, altering both of our lives forever.

My memories of Lila and this place fill my heart, and I am drunk with her love. I close my eyes. Remembering the sounds and smells of the farm, I find myself hypnotized by its aura. There isn't a day that passes without the memory of this special place I came to call home. And as God is my witness, there isn't a day that I forget the girl who arrived here several years ago, believing she was alone and had to take on the world by herself. I wasn't merely hiding from the past; I was hiding from my pain. Nothing about me was real. When the secrets started to unravel, although agonizing, they began to set me free. Lila and I had something colossal in common: secrets. Some people may refer to them as skeletons in the closet, and if that's really the case, well, they were haunting the hell out of me and begging to get out.

Our secrets are laced with lessons. They become our handbook of life, the river of truth, the glory of love, and the blessed existence of miracles. We are all only human beings, each having a physical body with a miraculous spirit within. We all experience the same things in this life: sorrow, joy, pain, and death. Whatever it may be, we are all on the path together.

I believe Lila is with me right now watching, and she blows on the back of my neck with the cool fall breeze. *Give me the courage,* I pray, *to go inside.* Will the aroma of her chocolate cake linger in the house? Will light still shine through the old cracked windows spilling God's heavenly essence? Will I fall to my knees, knowing that I have been truly blessed with her love? I pray for courage.

Never in my dreams would I have believed that those steps leading to the porch would be the very steps that I long to stand on now. This porch has a story, a life. It breathes with memories of truth and love. Time has left the imprint of our lives here forever, and I now stand bathing in those memories.

As Lila once said, "A person's soul holds the blueprint of their life, and with each step taken, we become closer to our own truth: the path to freedom, the path home, the path to love."

Chapter 1

I walked the long narrow corridor to the courtroom, willfully seeking attention by shaking my assets. The guards accompanying me, who I thought of as two little trolls, ran their hands across my ass, a clear indication of their twisted minds. Their eerily seductive smiles disturbed me, and each took turns winking at me, hoping the other wouldn't notice. As they held on to the firmest thing they had felt in years, I gave them my shifty grin and drew them in like prey, something I had learned and perfected on the streets. I'd met more than my share of losers, but these two could be bottled as insect repellant. Their uniforms barely fit, and the buttons on their shirts begged for mercy, held on by the very last thread. The waistbands of their pants hung on for dear life over their protruding potbellies.

With my arms pulled behind my back and wrists tightly handcuffed, I found myself not only uncomfortable, but I could hardly bear the idea of being vulnerable in a way that left me powerless. I could feel my heart beating heavily inside my chest and becoming even more rapid with every step closer to the courtroom. The blood pumping through my veins felt like kerosene that had been struck with a match. Survival instincts kicked in, and although fear wreaked havoc internally, I managed to look cool and composed on the outside.

I wish my mother were here, I thought to myself.

Looking around, I hoped to find a sign, letting me know she was right here with me, beside me. Angels had carried her home in the cold winter of 1996, just as I turned fifteen years old. As she drifted off into heaven, I drifted into hell.

In the weeks preceding her death, she tried to prepare me for a life without her. From the time I was a little girl, she had instilled in me a foundation of values and beliefs. This foundation gave her hope that I could survive and carry on after she was gone. Still, her fear of leaving me in a world without her was a fear far greater than her fear of death itself. It all seemed so unfair. She had once said, "The only certainty you will find in fair is a Ferris wheel. Life doesn't recognize fair. What it does recognize is what isn't." She was certainly right about that.

For me, it was a time of great sadness, and the uncertainty of a future without her left me frightened beyond anything I could have ever imagined.

My mother's name was Grace. She was incredibly beautiful and appropriately named for her inner beauty and strength. Unfortunately, months of intensive chemo and radiation had ravaged her frail body, leaving her skin gray and the cheeks of her face so sunken, she became almost unrecognizable. Since her passing, the little girl who once played like a child with all the freedoms of the world and who danced like a princess in her room no longer existed. With my heart hardened like stone and my soul blackened by the cruel realities of a sick world, the only thing recognizable about me since her death was my name.

I learned to survive, and I was tough, tougher than these two little fat trolls who probably sat alone on a toilet getting their jollies off in front of a centerfold. Their hands on my body felt like sewage entering my pores and creeping hideously into my soul with a foulness that only survives in hell. Their bodies spewed an aura of lust and a hunger for robbing innocence.

When I entered the courtroom, a shiver went up my spine, and the hair on the back of my neck stood at attention. No longer in my control, my future lay at the mercy of some smelly old judge, not to mention the court-appointed loser in charge of my case. The two trolls finally removed their dirty hands from my arms as we approached the desk before the judge's bench. They released the handcuffs from my wrist. I was free. For a brief moment, I wanted to run, but I knew the judge would be there shortly.

I would have liked to have made a better impression on the judge that morning, but the only clothes I had to my name were on my body. Tattered jeans and a T-shirt I had stolen from a Bon Jovi concert probably didn't constitute the most appropriate attire, but they were as dirty and worn as my soul. My long blond hair pulled back in a ponytail bounced when I walked, and after a summer in the sun, my golden brown skin covered the scars of the streets. With blue eyes that captured and entranced any young hot-blooded man, I knew exactly how to use my looks to get what I wanted or needed. Manipulation was the first lesson I had learned on the street.

Although I looked a bit rough around the edges, all eyes were on me, and I played everyone like a game. My court-appointed loser was seated and had been impatiently awaiting my arrival. Hell, I had spent the last few months in jail, and I looked better than he did. His plaid suit jacket, worn and wrinkled, looked as if he had just rolled out of bed. A stench of cigarette smoke permeated the air around him. Reaching into his jacket, he pulled out a small can of breath freshener and proceeded to drop his jaw, exposing a grotesque yellow tongue and smoke-stained teeth inside his big repulsive mouth. He squirted away, giving new meaning to the word *disgusting*, but what the hell? He was free. I took a chair beside him. His breath now freshened, he came within inches of my face and rudely instructed me to remain silent and not to speak unless spoken to.

A tall, handsome, and distinguished man appeared from a door behind the judge's bench.

"Everyone rise!" the bailiff shouted, nearly startling me off my chair.

You would have thought Jesus had come walking into the room by the way the bailiff and the two little trolls stood at attention.

"Please be seated," the judge said firmly as he lifted his black robe slightly to sit down.

He pulled his glasses down from atop his head and began to review documents placed in front of him. A man of middle age, he would have caught the attention of any woman, young or old. Piercing green eyes accented his dark hair, and his perfect olive skin made it hard to notice anything else in the courtroom. He took my breath away, not to mention my words, with his good looks. He glanced at me every so often as he continued to peruse the documents. I couldn't help but wonder what fate lay ahead of me.

Placing his glasses back into his lush dark hair and raising his head, he gazed at me with spellbinding green eyes. "Sophie, I have reviewed your case, and I'm addressing this situation with the deepest compassion and utmost concern for your future."

His voice matched that of his appearance: strong, affirming, and confident. His tone was low, but there was a kindness in his voice, something that I hadn't heard often.

With few words, he continued boldly, "I am placing you in the custody of your grandmother, Lila Mae Randolph."

I sat, stunned and confused. His words, flying like arrows, passed by me like the punch line of a joke going over my head; I knew I had heard it, but I didn't get it. For a brief moment, I found solace in the hope that he was joking until I noticed he wasn't laughing.

"She is a fine woman," he said. "After meeting and spending a considerable amount of time with Lila, I am certain she has your best interests at heart." He paused for a brief moment. The courtroom became deathly silent, the air so thick you could eat it.

Is this a joke? I thought to myself in disbelief.

My attorney looked at me with bewilderment, or as I would have said at the time, he had "a real stupid look on his face."

I examined the courtroom to see who I was becoming prisoner to, but outside of the judge, court reporter, and my attorney, there appeared to be no one else in sight. Concealing the fear that began to ravage my body, I quickly stood and kicked the chair out from under me. "Save the joke for April Fools, asshole!" I yelled hysterically to the judge. Becoming more volatile by the moment, I began screaming uncontrollably. "Are you crazy? Who made you God?"

My worthless loser of an attorney grabbed my arm and pulled me down in my chair. In an attempt to silence me and regain control, he began growling under his breath and sneering at me with his beady eyes. But nothing could control the fear and anxiety that rushed through every vein of my body. Everything in the room started spinning in slow motion, yet I was frozen in fear. The palms of my hands began to sweat, and my heart felt as if it were about to tear through my chest and jump onto the desk.

My attorney continued to tug on my arm. "Keep silent," he snarled.

"Don't touch me, you worthless pig!" I screamed crazily back at him. "I don't have a grandmother, you freak!"

For a brief moment, I thought I had been pulled into someone else's nightmare. This wasn't my life; it didn't resemble who I was or who I was supposed to be. I hoped that I would soon wake up and find Mom sitting beside me, softly telling me that everything was okay, that it had all been a bad dream. "Help me!" I begged Mom under my breath. "Please, please help me."

Shaken out of my skin, I wanted so badly to cry; I wanted my mother. I fought back the tears and searched the courtroom for any sign of her, but found none. Why had she left me? I could no longer do this alone. I sat down helplessly.

Throughout all of my hysteria, the judge had remained calm. Then he quietly proceeded. "Sophie, you do indeed have a grandmother, and she has been looking for you for a long time. If you choose not to live with her, I have no choice but to sentence you to the juvenile detention center for a period of one year." He paused for a moment.

Our eyes locked. Neither of us exchanged a word, but I sensed his seriousness.

"It's your choice," he stated thoughtfully.

I sat silently, not knowing what might lie ahead of me. Either way, I would be leaving the only life I had ever known, and my greatest fear was that the memories of Mom would also be left behind. Memories were all that remained; they were all I had.

My attention was drawn back to the courtroom and the judge who patiently awaited my decision. He put his pen down calmly and waited. I looked around the courtroom and noticed a clock on the wall. I could hear the ticking of the hand, and with each passing second, it seemed louder and louder. I began to feel as if I were a character in a slow-motion movie with a bomb ticking inside me, ready to explode. Suddenly, I was no longer in control. I laid my forehead down on the edge of the table in defeat, covered my face with my hands, and cried.

The judge watched with empathy, but said nothing. My attorney began shuffling his papers, which was even more annoying than his stupid looks and bad breath. After a few minutes, I could find neither the words nor the energy to speak, so I simply raised my head, wiped the tears from my face, and nodded to affirm the judge's decision.

"There's an old saying, Sophie," he said gently. "It goes, 'Hear me now, believe me later.' This is one of those times. You will be in the full legal custody of your grandmother and reenroll in school for a period of one year, at which time I will again review your case to see if any progress has been made. Your grandmother is giving you a chance to get the best out of life. I have faith she could be your saving grace, and I believe that's all you need—just a little grace."

He had no idea how profound those words were to me. He was absolutely right; all I needed was a little Grace.

"All rise," the bailiff shouted again.

Showing no emotion, the judge quickly exited the courtroom without saying anything further.

See what happens when your attorney is free? I thought sarcastically.

I had a feeling coming over me that I hadn't known before. The benevolent spirit of my soul and the sharpness of my tongue had both been silenced. I had been defeated. My mother once told me that in the middle of defeat, you may not realize that you have actually won. If you trust in him, you will never lose. I hadn't trusted him since he'd taken my mother away.

The creepy trolls approached the desk where I was seated and led me to an exit. They snickered and smirked while hurrying to rush me through the courtroom doors and down the hallway. At the end, a woman stood waiting. Though they didn't say so, I knew it had to be Lila Mae Randolph.

She looked strangely happy to see me. I, on the other hand, felt extremely strange seeing her.

I'm certain she must want something from me, I thought. *Why else would an old woman want a sixteen-year-old girl? She's crazy if she thinks I'm going to be free labor. I didn't just arrive from Maids R Us. She would be wise to wipe that sweet smile off her face because she has no idea who she's dealing with and what I have in store for her.*

As the creepy little trolls and I approached the woman, she continued smiling as if the smile were stuck on her face. The closer we got to her, the more I found myself surprised and speechless. She certainly wasn't what I had expected. Her smile was tender, not fake, and a gentleness shone through her eyes. Even the wrinkles that surrounded them added distinctive beauty that accentuated their ocean-blue color. Her full dark hair, laced with strands of silver, graced her face. Her dress—simple yet sophisticated—draped over her body like a glove. Although the dress was a little worn, she looked stunning. A small belt delicately wrapped around her waist added to her femininity, and a necklace with a cross hung from her neck. She looked old, or at least old to me, but her essence of grace and beauty outshone her age. Taller than me, she stood about five feet ten.

This isn't what grandmothers are supposed to look like, I thought. I had expected to find a little old fat lady with her hair in a bun, wearing a muumuu and an apron that read I Love Grandma.

"Hello, Sophie," Lila said softly, reaching to shake my hand.

"I don't know what your scam is, old lady, but I'm not buying it," I replied, angrily rejecting her welcome.

She remained gracious. "I understand you're confused, and I'm sorry that we're meeting this way."

"You don't understand anything about me," I said sharply. "Let's get one thing straight. I'm only going with you because that loser attorney of mine didn't do his job. I don't know what you're expecting, but get the picture of roses and daffodils out of your head."

Silenced, Lila bit her lip.

I certainly hadn't witnessed a grandmother like this before. She exuded an aura of inner beauty like a fragrant flower, and her essence filled the courtroom corridor. As she guided me out of the courthouse, we walked slowly side by side. I looked behind me, and to my surprise, all eyes rested upon her, not me. This was an imposter, I was sure! Or was I the imposter?

My emotions were scattered like leaves on a windy day in October. One moment, I wanted to run, and the next, this woman became more intriguing than I had ever thought possible. Everything was happening so fast. My journey had just begun. I walked down the steps of the courthouse with a woman I had never known, leaving all that had been familiar behind. With no idea of what lay ahead and curious beyond belief, I remained cool with fear.

As we approached Lila's old pickup, my fear shifted to a quiet and unspoken excitement. *What a classic!*

Memories of my boyfriend Gabe came rushing through my mind as I laid my eyes upon the old beast. Gabe and I had an appreciation, you could even say an obsession, for old cars and trucks, and I couldn't wait to tell him about this one. I hadn't seen him in months, since he got sentenced to prison, and God only knew when he would be getting out. It certainly wouldn't be early for good behavior as "good" didn't exist in his vocabulary. The old Ford was light blue in color, and the hood of the truck looked like the belly of a fat man with its age showing as rust had attacked the frame. Gabe had taught me how to drive a stick shift, and although I was a little rusty myself, I couldn't wait to get my hands on this baby.

"Do you know how to drive a stick shift, Sophie?" Lila asked kindly, possibly sensing a hint of my excitement as I examined the body of the old truck.

"I can drive anything."

"This was your grandfather's truck. I call it Old Blue." Lila chuckled. "Go on, get in. We have a long drive ahead of us."

Stepping up into the truck, I sat as close as possible to the door in an attempt to ignore the old woman. I had no intention of entertaining her with conversation and made it very evident by staring aimlessly out the passenger window. Lila drove like she had never driven a stick before. Every time she switched gears, it sounded like she was going to choke the hell out of the poor truck. At times, she would even curse and fight the stick as if in a personal battle she refused to lose.

There were very few things that brought Gabe excitement, but old cars and trucks—they were the real love of his life. He could take one apart and put it back together in an afternoon. I loved to watch him work. It was the only time he ever appeared to really be at peace.

I knew things were going to be different after Mom died, but in a million years, I could never have imagined the hell I would endure at the hands of a foster family. They appeared polished and refined on the outside, but were twisted and evil from within. I quickly learned that perception is never truth. The first thing they instilled in me was fear. The second thing I learned was survival.

They hurried me away from my mother's funeral after the service, and the torture began. After they thought they had broken me, they let me return to school. I knew how important my education was to my mother, so I tried to remain in school as long as I possibly could. But eventually, the abuse was far more than I could handle. My spirit was broken, along with my body, and I could no longer bear the pain, which was far worse than anything I had ever experienced in my life. I figured running anywhere would be better than staying there. They had taken every beautiful and wonderful memory of my life with my mother in River Crossing and shadowed it with guilt and shame. I ran, knowing that I could never return.

Eventually, I made my home on the streets of Lincoln, a large city fifty miles from River Crossing, where I met Gabe. We were both hustling on the streets and living wherever the day ended, usually under a bridge or in one of the city parks. Gabe and I had a mutual agreement: he would give me protection as long as I gave him my money. Actually, it wasn't an option. He owned the streets and anyone working them. Nobody messed with him, not even the cowardly local authorities, who went out of their way to avoid confrontation. In fact, they simply looked the other way.

Gabe's temper was as hot as his slender and sculpted muscular body. On his clean-shaven head, he replaced his hair with tattoos of gang symbols. He looked as dangerous as his volatile personality, and God have mercy on those in his path. Once his fuse had been lit, there was no turning back. On several occasions, I had found myself in his line of fire. I knew he never meant to hurt me, at least, not intentionally. Eventually, he would regain control, and the reality of what he had inflicted would soon be followed with sobbing and, ultimately, apology. He told me over and over again how special I was and how no other girl could make him feel the way I did. I believed him.

The bruises Gabe left on my body weren't permanent; the scars he carried were forever. From a young age, he had no choice but to take care of himself and his younger brother, moving from apartment to apartment as his parents drifted in and out of their lives. Spending the majority of their limited government-assisted income on drugs and living in and out of prison, his parents were habitually absent, both mentally and physically. A piece of Gabe had died when he held his mother in his arms and watched her die from a drug overdose, a memory that molded like concrete in his mind.

Looking out the window of Lila's pickup, I saw the last thing I recognized as we drove out of town, standing more brilliantly than ever: the old Steinhart Bridge. Mighty trees encompassed each side, and I recalled the sounds of their leaves rustling in the breeze, a hypnotizing lullaby of nature as Gabe and I fell asleep beneath them on many nights. I missed him deeply. The first opportunity to present itself, I would be sure to send a letter to the prison so he knew where I would be in the event he was released.

Lila checked the rearview mirror. "Are you all right, Sophie?" she asked softly.

I turned back to look at the city fading from view. A tear fell down my cheek, and I couldn't speak. My sentence had just begun.

Chapter 2

The ride, approximately 250 miles west from River Crossing to what Lila called the Great Plains of Nebraska, seemed long and awkward as we swerved back and forth on the old highway roads. At times, Lila attempted to make conversation, but I was deep within my own thoughts and spent most of the four-hour drive looking out the window wondering where the hell I was going and hoping to God she would just keep the old truck on the road.

The scenery, rather incredible in its own element, didn't change much: miles and miles of corn and bean fields for as far as the eye could see. I looked at Lila every so often, searching for any resemblance to my mother. To my surprise, she resembled her in so many ways that I found myself at times staring at her. I noticed her soft half smile, a characteristic my mother also possessed. She kept her lips together, smiling just a bit, as if she were trying to keep some of her excitement contained inside, just for herself.

"I hope you'll like the farm," Lila said kindly. "It's not for everyone. Your mother loved it when she was a little girl."

"I prefer the company of animals to people," I replied snottily.

"Then you'll like the farm," Lila replied with a hint of sarcasm.

It would be an understatement to say that this day had been unpredictable and overwhelming. With each mile closer to the farm, I began to feel strangely excited about returning to the same place in Nebraska where my mother had grown up as an only child. She was used to being alone and isolated. She didn't consider that a blessing, and as she got older, there were few things she liked about the farm. She joked that it was for animals. Still, I found myself wondering many times during the ride why she would leave the farm and never go back. Why had she severed ties to her family? Why had she kept me from knowing my grandparents? She had rarely spoken of Morton Falls. When she had, a change in her tone, as well as the look of sadness on her face, revealed more than words could ever tell.

On my thirteenth birthday, believing I was old enough to understand the circumstances leading to my existence and my father's absence, my mother shared her story with me. She had attended high school in Saint Paul, Nebraska, just a few miles from Morton Falls, where she met the young man of her dreams. She described her and my father as the couple everyone wanted to be. She was a cheerleader and he, of course, the football jock— all too cliché. It looked good on the surface, and for a while, the fantasy existed like a dream on steroids.

But when her boyfriend heard the news—shortly after their high school graduation—of my impending arrival, he quickly found his way out. Grace's dreams of becoming an artist with her own studio, among other things, would have to be put on hold. The shame and humiliation was more than she could bear. The gossip, infinitely common in a small town, tore at her spirit like a thousand knives.

I was born in Morton Falls on December 22, 1980, and within a few weeks of my arrival, we were on our way to River Crossing. Grace stuffed as much as she could into her 1967 Chevy Impala and left with no intention of ever returning. I often wondered why she looked sad when holidays, birthdays, and special milestones in our lives were upon us. Normally, these are special times shared and celebrated with family, but years continued to pass with no contact. Many times, I found her picking up the phone as if to call someone. But each time, the scenario always played out the same way, with her lowering her head in sadness and slowly replacing the phone back on the receiver. The past she kept hidden for so long left a noticeable emptiness in her heart. From time to time, she would get wind of deaths and other happenings from her hometown, but it was like throwing a glass against a brick wall: it shattered, but it never penetrated.

My father's absence since my birth left me with little or nothing to miss. In fact, I don't recall feeling a loss or sadness from not having him in my life. Life was amazingly comfortable and full without him. Mom told me he would always have a special place in her heart because he was part of something great: bringing life to both of us. After our conversation, I never gave him a second thought, and we never spoke of him again.

As Lila and I neared our destination, my head felt like it was about to explode. Thoughts and questions of the past filled my mind, and curiosity about an unknown future left me feeling uneasy, yet at times unexplainably excited. Luckily, our ride, even though long, would soon end at a farm situated just outside of Morton Falls. A sign on the side of the road read, Population 800.

"It's a small town," Lila said. She firmly gripped the steering wheel with both hands in her attempt to keep the old truck on the road.

She is undoubtedly the worst driver I have ever met. Trying to ignore her and anything she had to say, I kept my head deliberately turned away and looked pointlessly out the window.

"We're very close in this farming community, just like family," she said cheerfully.

Wow, eight hundred relatives! I can't wait to see what kind of drama and dysfunction this family has hiding in its closet. I continued to show no interest in her or the stupid history of this town. *No wonder Mom left.* I laughed to myself.

I thought River Crossing was small, but eight hundred people! That's not a town, that's a Friday night showing at Walmart. I had lived most of my life with my mother in River Crossing, a town rich in history. We loved all the old houses that lined the streets.

Hanging flower baskets with the deepest colors of purple and red decorated each porch, and gas lamps on the lawns created an array of warmth and color, a feeling of home portrayed as picturesque as a Norman Rockwell painting. The town's seven thousand residents weren't considered close, but they were definitely neighborly.

Situated along the Missouri River in eastern Nebraska, directly across from the Loess Hills of southwestern Iowa, River Crossing housed many parks. It wasn't uncommon to hear the laughter of children playing and dogs barking throughout the day. Evening sunsets fell upon the river like richly colored silk sheets upon a bed, and we could hear the sounds of night approaching, with frogs occupying the riverbanks and the moon quietly rising to take its place in the midnight sky. Our neighborhood was quiet, and the neighbors were friendly, always willing to lend a hand if needed. Everyone's pets roamed yard to yard, marking territory.

We had the smallest house on the block, with an umbrella of trees creating a feeling of security. The trees blanketed us with shade in the hot summer and protected us from the heavy snow typical of a cold Nebraska winter.

As we neared Lila's farm, she blessed me with a dissertation on each neighboring farm and the entire history of the family that lived there.

Jesus! I thought. *She's a frickin' walkin', talkin' genealogist.* Who could store that much irrelevant crap in their head?

Lila declined to acknowledge my lack of interest and continued rambling on. I wasn't quite sure, however, if her intentions were to be friendly or annoying. I confess that to me, it was the latter.

"Over here," she said, pointing out the window. "This is the homestead of Robert and Hilly Taylor. They're wonderful people. Robert was one of your grandfather's closest friends. They helped me manage the farm after Joe's death until I could find a good hired hand. I don't know what I would have done without them."

Blah, blah, blah.

Suddenly quiet, Lila hesitated for a moment. Chatty Cathy seemed to have lost her tongue. Her demeanor softened, and she asked sadly, "Did you know your grandfather's name was Joe?"

Although I wanted to remain silent, I could hear the tone of her voice and realized her cheerful manner had changed. Without speaking, I turned my head toward her and shook my head. I had never known my grandfather's name. I turned back to stare out the window. The silence suddenly became awkward.

It seemed odd and uncomfortable to have Lila speak of a grandfather and his passing. I had no knowledge of these two "grand" people. Mom had been highly successful at making sure that I didn't know anything about them. I assumed she must've had good reason for it. I felt nothing toward Lila and completely unattached from any emotion as she spoke of a husband lost, a husband she referred to as my grandfather.

"We're almost there," she said kindly. "I know it's been a long ride, and I'm sure you're hungry."

I didn't reply, but hell yes, I was starving. Just the mention of food made my mouth water.

The old truck began to slow, and Lila put her blinkers on, signaling to make a right turn. To the immediate right was a large farm. It was the closest farm to her home, yet her memory bank of millions of years of ancestry simply vanished, and she didn't say a word about it as we passed by.

Odd, I thought.

Although I had succeeded at ignoring her, I remained quite present during the drive, and I was curiously aware when Lila passed this particular farm in complete silence. She had never once taken her eyes off the road before her, but now suddenly, she had her head turned looking out her window, and we were almost in the ditch. There was a certain element of discomfort in her demeanor, and I wanted to stir the pot a little in what Lila referred to as a close family community.

"Whose farm is that?" I asked innocently.

"That would be the Gerards' farm," she replied quickly, with little emotion.

"Oh, I'll bet they're good friends of yours too," I said with a smile, though I meant it sarcastically.

"The good Lord calls upon us to love all of our neighbors," she replied, with a hint of bitter on her tongue.

Oh crap! I knew it. She's one of those spooky ladies who go door to door preaching the gospel, and once you let them in, you can't get them out. I've been sent to live with Tammy Faye Bakker. Gabe's gonna get a kick out of this when he reads about it. He hates this type. Several times a week, church missionaries would walk the streets targeting what they referred to as the poor homeless children. The last thing any of us wanted to hear would be a sermon on how great God is. Really! How great had he been to any of us? Gabe pulled a gun on one of 'em once, and they never set foot under Steinhart Bridge again.

We turned onto a long dirt driveway, and my thoughts about Gabe and about Lila's avoidance of her neighbor quickly escaped my mind when her farm came into view. When I awoke that morning, nobody knew me. For all I knew, no one cared. I had existed as a ghost for a long time, and I felt pretty sure I was satisfied with that. But suddenly, in one moment, looking at the farm, an excitement came over me that I hadn't felt for a long time. The closer we got to the house, the more I had this eerie feeling that Mom was there, watching us drive up. I imagined for a second that she would be waiting on the front porch with her arms wide open, and I would run to her with all the force of a hurricane, splashing into her beauty, and be home again. Sadly, it was just a dream.

Trees lined each side of the dirt road that led to the house. Branches formed a canopy over the top, and the cool fall wind blew among them. It felt as if the trees were welcoming us. Old, worn, and rusted farm machinery found its resting place beyond the trees as if a grave marker of the past. An overwhelming sense of peace emanated from this place, and my fear began to fade. An array of pleasantly unfamiliar emotions enveloped my senses. Large red buildings laced the landscape around the farm, and a tall windmill situated near what I later learned were the hog barns whistled as the wind blew upon it. The old oak trees were huge, and branches running like veins reminded me of a ghostly October night as they created a silhouette against the sky. Lila stopped abruptly to park, kicking the dust in the air, surrounding the truck into a brown cloud.

Once the dust cleared, I couldn't believe what I saw. It was larger than life. For a moment, I sat in awe.

"Well, go ahead and get out of the truck," Lila said kindheartedly.

"I will, I will!" I fired back, somewhat annoyed with her eagerness to take me captive.

I slowly stepped from the old truck, and looking upon the house, I took a deep breath. The air, finally clear of dust, smelled crisp, yet every so often, the breeze would bring in the distant smell of the cattle. Otherwise, it seemed perfect. With nothing to remove from the truck but my ass, I started up the steps.

The steps leading up to the porch were lined with flowerpots that created a vibrant color palette similar to the quaint neighborhood of River Crossing. The long porch wrapped around the front and east side of the house looked warm and welcoming, and at the end, a swing moved slightly back and forth as the breeze rolled across it. The three-story late-Italianate farmhouse gave the impression of wealth and clearly stood out as the most ostentatious of those that I had seen in the area. I pinched my arm to make sure I wasn't dreaming. Up until a few weeks ago, I lay cold, sleeping under a bridge, and today—well, I could hardly believe it myself.

"Come along," Lila said gently. "I'll show you to your room, and then you can wash up for dinner."

Another great surprise—food! I had been starving all day. The last meal I had attempted to eat, served early in the morning by the two little trolls, had quickly found its way into the trash can.

I followed Lila up the steps, and without warning, a large and very excited dog ran up behind me and nearly knocked me off my feet. He licked my face profusely and wagged his tail back and forth, making me feel welcome. I returned the affection with a pat on the head.

"He's friendly, sometimes too friendly," Lila said laughingly as he jumped all over me with excitement. "His name is Hunner, and he believes he's the keeper of the castle. I found him near the pond several years ago. I don't know how he got there. I find it hard to believe that someone would abandon a purebred Labrador retriever. I suppose it was meant to be, Sophie. The first thing you should know about me is that I don't believe in coincidences. I believe everything happens for a reason."

I continued to pet his chocolate-brown coat, and he licked my hands and arm as if they were coated with sugar.

"Get down, Hunner!" Lila told him firmly. "You can get acquainted later."

Lila's home looked welcoming, but so did the gingerbread house to Hansel and Gretel. A sign on the door read, "Enter this house with peace and love in your heart, and you will have entered a home."

I stepped inside the front door, and Hunner followed closely behind, making sure I wasn't out of his sight for long.

"Skedaddle!" Lila said, attempting to shoo him away.

My eyes turned to the ornate oak staircase leading to the second floor. I ran my hands along the wood. It felt smooth and reminded me of the times when Gabe and I went to car shows. I loved to run my hands across the polished hood of each car; the flawless beauty and shine were mesmerizing.

"It's beautiful, isn't it, Sophie?" Lila moved nearer to the staircase. "It took a local wood craftsman several years to complete.

He skillfully carved out every piece of wood as if each one were a work of art. I loved to watch him because he put so much of his heart into everything he created. Maybe one day you can meet him and compliment his work. I'm sure you'll like him. He used to be the local minister."

Seriously! I thought. *Now I get to meet Jim Bakker.*

"Well, let's not just stand here. Would you like to see the rest of the house?" Lila's voice held a breath of anticipation when she spoke.

"Sure," I replied, short and sweet, and began following her. Hunner walked quietly behind us. Every now and then, I found myself being distracted as Hunner pushed his nose into my ass. Lila seemed aggravated at times by his continued presence, despite her attempts to shoo him away, but I really didn't mind. In fact, I was sure I was going to prefer his company to hers.

Entering the sitting room, which looked like an elaborate parlor, I wondered if she had created a shrine or a sanctuary. I wasn't sure.

"This is my favorite room," Lila stated, noticeably excited. Her eyes lit up as she began picking up items and happily associating a memory with each.

I began perusing the room, but afraid I would break something if I picked anything up, I chose to just look.

By the way she picked up the picture from the mantle and held it tenderly, I realized the things in the room were more than material objects to her. I got the impression they were her treasures. She was as much an ornament in the room as the things she treasured. Rose-patterned wallpaper portrayed her style with an essence of femininity and serenity. Her most intimate keepsakes and photos precisely placed and present on every table and shelf suggested that this was a place close to her heart.

"Your grandfather thought I was crazy for saving these little trinkets. Some people may think they're just material things." She paused. "And for argument's sake, that's probably true." She smiled and said softly, "They trigger special memories that I hold close to my heart. They're helpful reminders. When you get old, Sophie, when you get to be my age, you need all the help you can get." She laughed. Gently picking up and gazing at pictures from the past, she recited a story about each.

Amazingly, I found myself interested. "Do you have any pictures of my mother?" I asked carefully.

If this old lady in fact was my grandmother, she would certainly have pictures of her daughter plastered all over the place, but I didn't see any, or at least any that I recognized.

"Come, dear," she replied, smiling as she approached the fireplace mantle.

I stood beside her, and we gazed at an array of eloquently decorated photo frames. My heart softened as she directed me to all the wonderful pictures of my mom. Pictures covered the entire mantle from left to right, creating a display of history from the time my mother was a baby until she graduated from high school. There was even an old faded one of her holding me after I was born. After Mom died, I was afraid that as time went on, I wouldn't be able to remember what her face looked like or what it felt like to touch her soft skin. Lila was right. All these little trinkets and pictures may not have meant crap to anyone else, but these pictures of my mother meant everything to me. My heart filled with joy, and I realized that Mom was exactly how I remembered her. She could never be forgotten.

"This one is very special to me." Lila reached for a photo centered directly in the middle of the mantle. "It's the only picture I have of the three of us together. We took it a few days before your mother left the farm. My friend Hilly insisted that we get a three-generation picture together." Lila chuckled. "Your mother refused to get in the shot at first. She wasn't much for pictures, but she knew Hilly well enough to know that she's a persistent old cuss and she wouldn't back down. Reluctantly, Grace finally gave in."

"She looks beautiful," I said sadly, running my fingers across the photo.

"She was so happy that day." Lila smiled softly, recalling the memories of the photo. "It's the last picture I have of your mother and one of the few that I have of you. If I would have known when she left..." She hesitated. "Well, if I could change the past, things might be different, but the reality is, I can't. I have to believe there's a reason for everything."

I could no longer deny that Lila was, in fact, my grandmother. Although the pictures were proof enough, when Lila talked of my mother's refusal to get in the shot, that confirmed everything. My mother hated having her picture taken.

While the prints brought joy beyond belief, they also brought pain beyond imagination. I tried hard to keep a poker face, but inside my heart, the joy quickly turned to sadness, and I wanted nothing more than to fall to the floor and bawl. However, a master at concealing my emotions, I hoped Lila wouldn't notice me standing painfully quiet.

Lila reached for a particular photo from the mantle and placed it close to her heart.

"What does that picture remind you of?" I asked curiously. The image was that of an attractive middle-aged woman sitting on a log by the pond.

Lila smiled sweetly, but said nothing—quite unusual for someone who seemed eager to talk about everything. Quietly, she placed the picture back on the mantle.

The silence left me curious.

"Let's move on. There are many rooms to see." Lila left the room swiftly.

Moving down the hallway with Hunner trailing directly behind us, we approached an incredible room with mahogany walls and a richly carved desk that enveloped most of the space. I could smell the wood, which gave me a sense of being in the forest.

"This is the library," she said proudly. "It was your grandfather's favorite room." She seemed happy as she spoke of him and gazed at his chair as if he might still be sitting there. "He sat in that chair every evening reading the local *Herald* and meticulously planning out each day. He was such an organized man, sometimes to a fault, but with many things to do, he spent much of his time and thoughts on the details of each day. We were very different. He planned each day, but I believed the day would plan me. You never know what's going to happen on a farm."

We left the library and headed for the next room on the tour. It wasn't hard to identify. My nose identified it right away—my favorite place in a house—the kitchen. It was huge. In my entire life, I had never been in a kitchen this big. An adjoining mudroom housed a wash sink and trays of egg cartons. Immediately outside the mudroom, a door opened to a small brick sidewalk leading to a chicken coop. Lila insisted that we walk to the coop so she could show me the chickens. The chicken coop was small, with shelves harboring rows of chickens sitting upon piles of straw.

"Walk on in." Lila nudged me gently.

"Are you kidding?" I replied sharply. I had no intention of entering.

Lila laughed and entered the coop before me. "They won't hurt you," she said, as if to coax me in.

Pinching my nose to avoid the wretched smell, I slowly stepped inside to shut her up. The stink was bad, but the sound was even more dreadful.

"Watch out for this one." Lila pointed to one of the hens. "She'll peck ya! She's a feisty old bird. I've had her for a long time. The other hens keep their distance. You always have one in the bunch." Lila chuckled.

I stepped out quickly, not amused by her comment. Surely, she wouldn't put me in this stink pit with a bunch of pecking maniacs.

"Rain or shine, we get eggs every morning," Lila said. "That'll be your job from now on, Sophie. That used to be your mother's job, you know," she said it cheerfully, as if it were somehow pleasing.

Now I know why she left this hell hole, I thought to myself. *If I had to stick my hand under some chicken's ass every morning, I'd be packing along with her.*

The only way I would get in that torture chamber again was with a gun.

Back in the kitchen, my mind became easily distracted with the aroma of Lila's baked bread sitting on the counter. I was hungry, and if we didn't eat soon, I'd be collecting eggs from one less chicken's ass.

All that remained for us to see on the main floor was a dining room, which Lila seemed eager to pass.

"Since Joe died, I really haven't had a reason to put this room to use," she said with a hint of sadness. "I do most of my entertaining on the porch anymore. Besides, Robert and Hilly are just about the only company I have these days, and they prefer the outdoors to this stuffy old room."

A centerpiece of fresh flowers sat on the big oak table, but the rest of the room smelled old and stale, giving the impression that it hadn't been frequented in years. An absence of life filled the room, and the flowers on the table would have had more company in a cemetery.

"Usually, I eat on the porch. But with the weather changing and becoming cooler, it's about time for me to move back into the kitchen. It feels much lonelier when you set at a big table for yourself."

"Have you tried a smaller table?" I asked with a bit of smartass on my tongue. *Maybe the chickens could join her.* I laughed to myself.

By the look on her face, I could see she didn't find my humor as funny as I did. With no reply from Lila, we left the dining room and proceeded to the second floor. As we began to make our way up the oak staircase, I noticed Lila moved slowly, stopping to bring her feet together on each step. At the pace she was moving, it would be tomorrow before we reached the second floor. Hunner continued to shove his nose up my ass in an attempt to get to the top, and my patience was wearing thin. After what seemed like an eternity, we finally reached our destination.

Lila stopped for a moment, holding on to the handrail, and paused to catch her breath. "These steps are going to kill me," she grumbled.

Well, if the steps don't kill her, she'll probably starve on the way up, I thought.

"The room to your left was your grandfather's," she said, still trying to catch her breath.

A tall oak headboard was meticulously carved with scrolling leaves and acorns, and the room exuded a feeling of masculinity. A large wingback leather chair sat in one corner, and beside it, a small table where his reading glasses and pipe still remained. You could still smell the aroma of tobacco in the room. A large bookcase housed hundreds of books, and reading material still lay on his table along with his riding boots beside the chair.

"Sometimes when I come in here, the room feels alive with his presence," Lila said with an air of regret in her voice. "I haven't touched a thing since he's been gone."

"Do you think he's coming home?" I asked jokingly, as if to make fun of her.

"Well, if he does, you'll be the first person to see him," she fired back. "You'll be staying in the room across the hall from his."

Holy crap! The old bat has a sense of humor!

Lila smiled, as if boasting about her sassy comeback.

If she were a peacock, her feathers would be up my ass.

We proceeded to the right of the staircase.

"This is my room, Sophie," she said. She opened the door slightly, allowing me a peek inside.

I caught a glimpse of a four-poster brass bed, the most incredible bed I'd ever seen in my life. Brass moldings of cherubs decorated both the headboard and footboard, and the crisp white linens and hand-sewn pillowcases created an essence of antiquity. A nightgown lay at the foot of the bed, and slippers were on the floor beside it. Perfume bottles, along with several pictures, stood atop her dresser. Lila swiftly pulled the door shut, and I felt unwelcome in her room.

My thoughts turned to the obvious. Why would two people who were married have bedrooms apart from one another? Was there a story here? I'm sure there was, but I wasn't going to ask. Not now, anyway.

The other two bedrooms across from the staircase housed what Lila called her guest rooms. Hunner stood quietly by one of the bedroom doors. His large brown eyes looked intently at me, seemingly trying to tell me something, so without hesitation, I went to the room. Looking in, my excitement grew, and I could hardly hide my emotions.

"This will be your room, Sophie," Lila said tenderly.

"A bed!" I shouted excitedly. I lost all sense and ran to the tall brass bed, covered by a hand-quilted comforter. Large overstuffed pillows lay against the headboard, with a beautiful doll placed gently amid the pillows. Looking around the room, I began to notice personal belongings and pictures of my mother. For a brief moment, I would have sworn I even felt her in the room with me. I imagined her sitting at the writing desk or lying in this wonderful bed. I noticed her pom-poms from her days as a cheerleader and pictured her jumping up and down at a football game. I felt her welcoming me into her room.

I turned to Lila. "Was this her room?" My eyes welled up with tears, and a part of me felt like I was home again with my mother.

"Yes, it is, Sophie," Lila said sympathetically. "Yes, it is."

Continuing to study every detail of the room, I tried to fight back the tears. I looked at the bed as if I were looking at a sanctuary of my mother's love. I sank my face down into the pillow and took several deep breaths in and out. The linens felt so crisp, and their fresh smell lingered in the room.

"Nothing else smells like linens on the line," Lila assured me. "The country air beats any fabric softener."

Hand-sewn pillowcases on the bed matched those that I remembered as a young girl. My mother had been a skilled seamstress. She made most of our clothing, as well as many other items in the house, including curtains and bedding. As a special surprise, she made clothes for my dolls at Christmastime. Each dress was crafted with incredible detail, and every stitch was undeniably sewn with love.

I hadn't slept in a real bed for over a year. The last time I slept with Mom, we were wrapped up in each other's arms watching a scary movie, gorging ourselves with popcorn, and then laughing ourselves to sleep. Reminiscing for a moment, I could no longer hold back the flow of tears. They ran down my cheeks and dripped from my chin to my shirt.

Lila gently placed her hand on my shoulder. Her touch evoked an emotion inside of me that felt good and genuine, but had been forgotten and lost long ago. She smiled tenderly as I examined the objects in the room and watched patiently, without a word. I experienced a sensation of getting to know Mom all over again, the young, innocent girl with the wind in her sails. Pictures of her paintings were posted all over the walls, and the memory of those alone took my mind back home. The inside of our house had had Mom's paintings on display in every room. Hippie-style beads and colored lightbulbs were mixed with contemporary furniture and art. Given its eclectic and artistic nature, I sometimes wondered if we were living in a house or an art studio.

Painting lived in my mother's soul as her first love. That her talent was hugely overlooked in a small town where an eye for art went no further than a tattoo of a naked woman on a fat man's arm seemed shameful. However, her paintings weren't ignored altogether. They were admired and appreciated in the neighboring town of Lincoln, which we always referred to as the Big City. The canvas would come alive as she delivered a piece of herself with each stroke of the brush. On many occasions, it appeared to me as if she had left her body and stepped inside the painting. She described it as spirit guiding each stroke, with her merely being the instrument. It sounded incredibly strange to me, yet believable. I watched her in awe, hoping that someday I, too, would be able to find that special talent within myself. From time to time, she would sell a few of her paintings for extra money, and we would treat ourselves to ice cream.

Everything in this room screamed of my mother, and even though it made me sad, it also gave me the greatest joy.

Every room in Lila's home was exquisitely decorated. Each room we had seen had filled my eyes with delight and curiosity. Describing them as if she had lived in each one for a lifetime, she embraced the rooms with conversation of her memories, an array of her own personal life's details. Throughout the house, lace curtains blew gently as the crisp fall wind welcomed itself inside. This wasn't just a house, and these weren't just rooms. There was a life given to them.

The farm, Hunner, and this home were far more than I could ever have imagined. Looking back now, I was aware that my mother and I didn't have much. In fact, we had very little. The true blessing was that we didn't know it, or at least I didn't. With only one income and a child to support, Mom was a thrifty shopper who frequented many auctions, garage sales, and even the local thrift stores to buy sewing materials and items needed for the house. Many of the storekeepers in town took pity on us and gave extra discounts at the register, which was not at all unheard of in a small town where compassion was still alive and well among good, honest Christians.

Lila and I finished the tour of the barns, and after a quick dinner, we were both exhausted. With each yawn coming closer together, I was ready to call it a day. I had woken up in the morning in a filthy jail cell, met a grandmother I had never known, and found a new friend in Hunner. Now I would be sleeping in a real bed in my mom's room on a farm in the middle of nowhere Nebraska. That was a lot to handle in one day.

We headed upstairs to our bedrooms. Hunner followed and took his place beside my bed.

"You'll find a nightgown in the bottom drawer." Lila pointed toward the dresser. "Good night, Sophie," she whispered. Turning the lights off, she waited a few moments for a response. When I didn't answer, she exited the room and closed the door behind her. We laid the day to rest.

The recent memories of sleeping alone and cold haunted me. Some nights had been so cold that I begged God to let me die. I pleaded with him to take me home. Lying here, as I looked at this home and this room, I wondered if he had answered my prayers. Surely not! He hadn't done anything for me before. Why would he start now?

My mom used to tell me, "Yesterday was a memory, today is a gift, and tomorrow there's hope." With that, I ended the evening as I settled into bed, feeling as if I had landed in a heavenly cloud in an uncloudy sky.

I closed my eyes, but my inquisitive nature and Hunner's loud snoring kept me awake for a while. I wondered why Mother would leave such an incredible home and never come back. More than one mystery occupied this farm, and I finally fell asleep with one question on my mind: *What mystery do I solve first?*

Chapter 3

I awoke in the morning to a rooster crowing. He sounded as if he were trying to cough up a trumpet. Hunner had snored like an old man all night. I hoped there was at least one animal on this farm that would be less annoying.

My frustration was short-lived, however. The sun's rays shone through the curtains, warming my bed, and the intoxicating aroma of breakfast filled the air. After falling off to sleep the night before, I slept comfortably, only waking to throw a pillow at Hunner every now and then. There were no nightmares, and my only fear was that I would begin to like it here. Nothing is forever, and I couldn't handle any more disappointments.

Lying with the sun shining on my skin, I began thinking about the girl I was before Mom died and the girl I had become. I was so ashamed, and I hoped that every man who had laid his hands on me would burn in hell. I wasn't the girl that I wanted to be or the girl that Mom hoped I'd be. I was glad she wasn't here to see who I had become.

I missed the beauty of her light upon this earth, and I had begged God many times to bring her back to me, but to no avail. Before she died, I sat quietly beside her bed gently sweeping the hair from her face and stroking her cheeks. At the moment she drifted off into the heavens, a radiant glow swept across her face. In an instant, she appeared smiling, with skin as pink as a rose and soft as the petals. I kissed her on the forehead and cried. I couldn't breathe. She was gone. Gone from me forever, and in that moment, I was gone too.

I had buried Grace Ann Randolph on a Monday in a beautiful cemetery on the outskirts of River Crossing. Known as Three Oaks, the cemetery was named appropriately for the large oak trees that shadowed the entrance of the burial grounds. Together, we had planned every detail of her funeral, picking out a modest casket, baby blue in color with a white satin lining, and a stone bench as a grave marker.

"Once I'm gone," she said in an attempt to comfort me, "come and sit with me on the bench and tell me all about your day."

I tried that many times, but anger's bitterness silenced my tongue, and tears replaced words. Sometimes, I would sit on the bench, and the breeze rolling across my shoulders felt as if she were wrapping her arms around me. Unfortunately, it couldn't compare to or ever take the place of her touch. When she died, I knew I could never live another day as I had known it. I died along with her, and from that day forward, I could only live to exist.

Sounds of pots and pans clanking in the kitchen were a welcoming noise; the rooster, however, needed to be shot. I lay sinking deep into the bed that cradled me the night before. Lying patiently beside the bed, Hunner stared at me with his big brown eyes and panted heavily, waiting for me to retreat with him to the kitchen. Even though I wanted to step from my cloud and follow the aroma, I closed my eyes and pinched myself to make sure that I wasn't still dreaming. Opening my eyes, I reached down and patted Hunner on the head. He looked at me as if he knew my pain. I wanted to hold this moment forever. Moments like these could be taken away so quickly. *You have to be careful not to get used to them*, I told myself.

The chill of fall air was moving throughout the house, and I shivered as Hunner and I scampered down the stairs. Nearing the kitchen, I could hear Lila humming and the scurrying of her slippers as she shuffled across the old wooden floor. I stood outside the door, listening to the softness of her voice and the sadness that accompanied her like a deep cello. The melody she hummed was somehow mesmerizing.

I slowly opened the door and stepped into the kitchen.

Lila turned and smiled at me. "Good morning," she said, pointing her spatula toward the table. "Have a seat."

"Good morning," I replied quietly.

"Did you sleep well?"

"It was fine."

"I hope Rosco didn't wake you." She laughed, knowing full well that I knew exactly who Rosco was. "He's just part of the farm. It's something you'll either grow to love or grow to despise."

I pulled out a chair from the large kitchen table and sat down. Hunner rested beside me on the floor and stared up at me, as if to remind me that he was there for any leftovers.

"Stop it!" I growled under my breath, but to no avail. My level of tolerance peaked when his tongue began protruding and hanging down one side of his jaw. He reminded me of my attorney, which escalated my annoyance even further. "Go away!" I shouted, louder and more convincing. He scurried around the table and came to rest beside Lila, a safe distance away from me.

"I've probably spoiled him a bit," Lila confessed. "I found him one evening as I was walking to retrieve the mail and heard whimpering in the tall grass near the pond. I disregarded the noise and continued on to the mailbox, but on my way back to the house, I heard the whimpering again and decided to investigate. I walked closer to the pond, and resting among the tall grass, I spotted a small puppy. He was adorable. I walked the banks of the pond looking for his mother or any other puppies that might have been abandoned, but there was nothing. I assumed that he had wandered off from his mother because I couldn't believe that someone would just leave him there alone without food or shelter.

"I surely didn't need another animal to tend to, especially with no help on the farm and endless work waiting for me, but when

I looked into his little brown eyes, I was hooked. I couldn't take my eyes off him as I carried him back to the farm, and before we returned, I had already named him Hunner. He's been my constant companion ever since. Evenings were a little more bearable and less lonely as we snuggled close to one another. Our first visit to the veterinarian for shots revealed his surprising pedigree. That's when I found out he was a purebred Labrador retriever. I guess I'll never know how he really came to be on the farm, but whatever the case, I believe that God had something to do with bringing him into my life."

"Do you really believe God has something to do with everything?" I asked sarcastically.

"Pretty much," Lila replied, without blinking an eye.

The table was graced with an amazing selection of breakfast foods. My stomach growled in anticipation. A variety of jams were spread out before me, most of which appeared to be homemade.

Lila finished at the stove and sat down directly across the table from me. When I reached for my fork, she gently placed her hand on top of mine. "I like to say grace first."

"Grace," I said sarcastically, a tiny smirk escaping my lips. I couldn't wait to get my hands on the food.

Lila bowed her head. "Dear Lord, we thank you for this food and the beautiful morning that you have blessed us with. Thank you for answering my prayers and bringing Sophie home. Amen."

Many things were unfamiliar to me on this farm, and praying was just another one. Often, I had wanted to pray, but I couldn't. I wasn't just angry with God, I hated God. Where was he when I needed him? He only answered the prayers of those seeking self-gratification. I knew plenty of men whose prayers he answered while watching me live through hell.

Without conviction, I went through the motions, and after grace, I ate like it could be my last meal. My mouth constantly occupied with food, I said little. Lila reminded me every so often to slow down as food was plentiful on the farm. But I took nothing for granted. I wasn't so sure it wouldn't really be my last meal, so I continued to eat until I was almost sick. "Thanks," I said appreciatively.

We both sat uncomfortably quiet. After I had stuffed myself like a pig, the only thing that escaped from my mouth was an occasional belch.

Lila acknowledged my thank you with a nod and a half smile and began removing dishes and food from the table. She approached the sink, and the morning sun that shone upon her through the kitchen window took a backseat to her natural beauty. I noticed that in her presence, everything around her seemed quite mute and meaningless. My mother had a similar quality, and I found myself consumed with questions.

Turning to me, Lila appeared as if she had been holding her breath, waiting to release everything she was about to say. When she began to speak, the words spilled out as if each word were chasing the other from her mouth. "There's so much I want you to know, Sophie," she said with a contained excitement. "I just don't know where to begin." She paused. Laying the dishrag down on the table, she sat across from me and proceeded. "I know you must have a lot of questions. I'm sure we both have a lot of curiosity about each other, and since we're going to be living together for the next year, well, I hope we can make the best of it." She smiled. "My wish is that one day we can at least be friends."

She was right about one thing: I definitely had a lot of questions. Although she spoke convincingly, I was a long way from trusting anyone and had little interest in a friendship with someone my mother desperately ran away from years ago. Struggling for a response, I said nothing.

"I guess we can take baby steps," Lila said sadly, noticing my willful intent to remain silent. She picked up the dishrag, returned to the sink, and began drying dishes. For a few minutes, I sat awkwardly at the table wondering if it was okay to get up and leave or if I should wait to be excused. Finally, I pushed my chair slowly away from the table.

Lila stopped drying dishes and turned toward me. I could see that she had been crying. "You were beautiful, so beautiful," she said gently, her voice shaking and her eyes again welling up with tears. "Your mother counted all of your fingers and toes, and we both cried." Lila laughed a little to herself, but still fought her tears as she tried to speak. "I watched Grace bring you into this world and give you life. But the real truth, Sophie, the real truth is, you gave life to her." She stopped for a moment.

Although I was wary of her, she had captured my interest, and I wanted her to go on.

"Your eyes were a beautiful blue, just like your mother's, and you had fine blond hair that felt like rich silk. She kissed you on the cheek and held you close to her heart and stared at your face as if she were trying to record the moment in her mind to hold for a lifetime. I held that moment and your face in my mind for all these years." She paused. "You may not know me, but I have never forgotten you. I just want you to know that I'm glad you're here." That said, she quickly returned to her work in the kitchen.

A part of me wanted to make her hate me, but the kindness and honesty in her words were making it extremely difficult. I was careful about letting my guard down. Evil comes in all kinds of packages, and as the old saying goes, "You can never judge a book by its cover."

"God has given us a beautiful October morning," Lila said as she gazed out the kitchen window. "We have a lot to talk about, but that will come in time. I don't want to push you, Sophie. I know you've been through a lot."

With a full stomach and a new day ahead of me, I swiftly ran to my new room, removing my nightgown on the way. I quickly changed into the clothing I had worn the day before, and Hunner and I bolted from the house like two children headed for a playground.

"Don't forget the chickens," Lila yelled from the kitchen.

Damn! I was hoping she was kidding last night, but apparently not.

Stepping outside, I noticed the leaves raining from the trees. They displayed a palette of colors unmatched by anyone other than God. Their colors of orange, red, and gold fell like feathers upon the earth, a spectacular dance of Mother Nature. This place was quiet, nothing like the city. You could hear the wind move through the branches of the trees as if it were music. Many nights in the city park, I would find the biggest tree to lie beneath. I dreamed of what it would be like if I could mimic its strength. The trees had weathered many storms and survived even the harshest cold and wind, yet they still stood strong, with branches reaching valiantly to the heavens.

The long dirt road situated between two cornfields leading from the farm to the highway invited Hunner and me to take a walk on this cool October morning. We had no more taken a few steps from the porch than I heard a screeching sound and then the abrupt slam of the porch door.

"I gotta get that fixed," Lila grumbled to herself.

Hunner and I turned quickly to see Lila standing on the porch.

"I've got chores to do, Sophie, so you'll have to fix your own lunch today," she said apologetically, yet sternly, with a no-nonsense smile. "I've wrapped some things and left them in the fridge. And don't forget to feed Hunner. His food is in the barn by the pig lot. Robert and I will be working late into the evening to get the crops out of the fields, but I suspect you'll be able to take care of yourself. There's a basket for gathering eggs in the mudroom, and if you run out of crates, there are more in the cellar." She continued to bark orders as Hunner and I turned and headed for the barns. "There's always work to be done on a farm, Sophie," she yelled from a distance. "We'll talk about your chores tonight at dinner." Her voice faded out as she stepped up into the tractor.

Chores! I grunted. I knew she had something up her sleeve.

Hunner and I embraced the day by spending hours of enjoyment running through the magical maze of cornfields. In the afternoon, we climbed a ladder to the second story of an old weathered and worn red barn that housed the hay. Two doors unlatched and opened to the outside with an amazing view of the entire farm. I sat down and swung my legs over the edge, looking out at the miles and miles of golden fields and the endless blue sky. Hunner sat quietly next to me, and we both bathed in the cool afternoon sun. I found myself becoming fond of the old mutt, and even though he continually annoyed me by shoving his nose into my ass, he began to grow on me. Silenced by our exhaustion, we glanced at each other every so often to acknowledge each other's presence. I felt unfamiliarly happy and safe.

I could see both the Taylor and Gerard farms from the upper level of the barn. But what was even more exciting was something that looked like a body of water situated between the two. You couldn't see it from the road, and it didn't appear big, but it looked intriguing. Hunner and I quickly retreated from the barn and headed out to investigate. Coming closer, I found a path from the road leading through the tall grass directly to the most incredible body of water I had seen in a long time, a pond. Cottonwood trees lined the outer banks, and the surface water rippled with a few breaths of the wind. An old log that rested beside the pond seemed a perfect place to sit and gaze at the beauty of this space. I took a seat, while Hunner jumped in and out of the water, playfully splashing and swimming around. Every time he jumped on shore, he shook the water off his coat— hence, soaking me.

It wasn't long before we tired of the pond and headed back to the farm. I spotted the infamous rooster as we neared the house. Suddenly, my rebellious nature took over. I felt militant, and I had an idea. "Come on, Hunner," I shouted, running eagerly to the mudroom.

I grinned from ear to ear. It was my turn to show this benevolent little cock-a-doodle-doo who was boss. Grabbing the egg basket from the mudroom, I departed quickly for the chicken coop, with Hunner following a few steps behind. I entered carefully. The smell alone was enough to knock a buzzard off a dead wagon. How the hell was I going to withstand the smell and remove the chickens from their nest in an attempt to rob them of their young? I needed a plan.

Running swiftly back to the kitchen, I grabbed a dishrag from the counter, draped it just above my nose, and tied it securely around my face. I looked badass. Officially declaring myself the egg bandit and dangerously armed with a pair of tongs, I returned to the chicken coop ready for battle. Hunner followed, but refused to go any farther than a few feet from the chicken coop door. Even though I tried to coax him inside with me, he wisely refused, parking himself firmly in the grass.

Once I got inside, fear took a backseat to my agenda of revenge, and I began poking chickens with the tongs, moving them from their nests, and robbing them of their eggs. For every egg I safely placed in the basket, I broke three. All hell broke loose, and the chickens went crazy. Wings were flapping, and feathers were flying. It looked as if a pillow fight had ensued. After a while, I couldn't see much of anything, except for dust and feathers, so I quickly escaped.

"Woo-hoo!" I shouted, ready for my next phase. "Let's go get him, Hunner."

Trying to run gracefully around the farm with the basketful of eggs wasn't easy. I have never claimed to have much grace; in fact, I was far more the klutz than the ballerina.

"Here, Rosco! Here, Rosco!" I began calling for him sweetly as if he were an adored pet.

All of a sudden, from behind the barn, I spied the noisy little cock coming around the corner. Hunner swiftly followed my every step, and we ran like the wind chasing after Rosco. I began throwing eggs from the basket, and each time I got one close enough to knock him off his little bird feet, I shouted as if I had won the lottery. Throwing my arms into the air, I performed a victory dance in celebration of defeating the pesky little cock. It was the most fun I had had in months, but of course, at the expense of Rosco.

The rest of the afternoon we terrorized the chickens and pigs by chasing them incessantly, wearing ourselves into exhaustion. When evening was upon us, we lay in the grass under a large oak tree, and I took in all the smells of the cool October breeze. It was as refreshing as crisp linen sheets in the wind.

I couldn't let Lila know how amazing this day made me feel. I believed that once you get soft, people will take advantage of you. My heart had been weary yesterday when I arrived at the farm, but today, I felt a bit like I had room to breathe.

This place was filled with memories from a life my mom once lived. Although I had no idea what had happened to make her leave and never return, I knew that she still must have loved this place and must have thought of it often. Was the sadness I saw in her eyes from the remembrance of her life here on the farm? She was a nature lover, and she showed that love by teaching me to honor and appreciate everything God had bestowed upon us. She used to say that God had always intended for us to live in his creation of beauty and wonder. The farm was a perfect example of that.

I thought of our evening walks to the park. Revisiting these in my mind gave me great joy. For me, it was the most anticipated event of the day, an unforgettable time of simply being next to her, holding her hand, and looking upon her as if she were an angel sent just for me.

Now I was on the farm where Mom's journey had long since ended, while my journey was just beginning.

Before we knew it, nighttime was upon us. After ravaging the refrigerator, Hunner and I patiently waited on the porch for Lila.

I could see the lights and hear the sound of the tractor coming up the road. I couldn't believe that it was nearly 11:00 p.m., and Lila hadn't taken a break all day.

She stepped down carefully from the tractor and began approaching the porch. Yesterday, I hadn't noticed how tired her face looked, or was it sad? I couldn't tell. Today, I saw a woman worn. She moved slowly, as if she were feeble and sore. Her jeans and flannel blouse were dust ridden from the fields. Her hair was pulled back in a bandanna and topped with a rancher's hat to protect her face from the sun earlier in the day. The cold October wind had surely neglected to keep her young.

Approaching the house, she pulled off her gloves. Even as tired as she must have been, she reached out to me with such kindness. Placing the back of her calloused and dry hand on my cheek, she smiled. "Your cheeks are red from the sun. Did you have a good day?" she asked as we walked into the house.

"It was okay," I replied, without emotion, keeping out any hint of pleasure.

The screen door screeched and slammed loudly behind us as we entered the house. "Damn, that's annoying," Lila commented. "I've gotta get that fixed. I hope you found yourself something to eat."

"I fried up some eggs."

"I apologize for leaving you here alone, but work on a farm never ends, especially around harvest time," she said, sounding exhausted.

Hunner and I stood in the foyer, our faces guilt-ridden from our earlier assault on the rooster. An awkward silence ensued.

"Sophie, it's been a long day. Let's move along to bed. We'll talk about chores at breakfast tomorrow."

I was hoping that she would forget about the whole chore thing, but it hadn't slipped her mind like it had mine.

"We'll go into town and buy you some clothes tomorrow," she said. "You'll need some work clothes as well. This old farm takes mercy on no one." She slowly moved toward the staircase.

Watching her climb the stairs to her bedroom, I began to see the strength in her and wondered how she had lasted on the farm for so long. One thing was becoming certain to me: Lila had traits like my mother's. She had her smile, her kindness was unmatched, and her gentleness was honest. She was my mother's mother...she was my grandmother. It felt good to let my guard down a little. *How the hell am I ever going to explain the egg incident?* I thought to myself.

The next morning came quickly, but another wonderful night of sleeping on my cloud prepared me for the day. Pots and pans rang a pleasant sound in my ear, drawing me like prey into the kitchen.

"Good morning," Lila greeted me, as I shuffled into the kitchen and sat at the table. She placed a plate in front of me.

I discreetly breathed in the intoxicating aroma of bacon and scrambled eggs. "Hi," I replied quietly, picking up my fork. Before digging in, I looked up at Lila. "Thank you."

A small smile lit up her eyes. "You're welcome, Sophie." She turned back to the stove, dished up her own plate, and took the seat directly across from me. "The chickens must be a little nervous with new company on the farm. Eggs were scarce this morning." She poked her fork into her scrambled eggs.

I lowered my head and began shoveling food into my mouth in an attempt to conceal my guilt.

I was relieved that she didn't ask me about my past. I wasn't ready to talk about it, and Lila seemed to understand this. I desperately wanted to ask her why she looked so sad all the time, but curbed the impulse. She was obviously going out of her way to respect my privacy. At the very least, I could do the same for her.

Clearly, we both had secrets.

Chapter 4

The sun rose gloriously over the distant hills each morning, beckoning the rooster to wake all on the farm. Crowing began precisely as the sun's rays shed their light over the land and continued until Rosco saw some type of movement from within the house. Often, it was a shoe pummeled at him, accompanied by, "Shut up, you mangy bird!" This worked for a while, but when I realized foul language and flying objects couldn't quiet the persistent little creature, I was forced to accept him. I even began to like him. He, on the other hand, wasn't so quick to warm up to me. He scurried away swiftly at the mere sight of me. I assumed the whole egg incident was still fresh in his mind. However annoying, he became a constant reminder that I was still here and welcome.

Chores became tolerable, and routine began to settle in. Lila made a weekly checklist of my duties and put it under a magnet on the refrigerator door. She knew the fridge was the place I frequented most and the one place where I couldn't escape seeing the list. Gather eggs in the morning, put fresh straw in the chicken coop, feed Hunner, give scraps to the cats, bring fresh water for the horses—on and on and on it went. I often argued with her about the list, but Lila assured me that nothing on it would kill me. I didn't like her humor at times, but I put up with it.

The sounds of pots, pans, and dishes being used echoed throughout the house, and the smell of breakfast lingered, dragging me unwillingly from the warmth of my bed to the cold wooden floors. The sound of farm machinery was distant outside, and the cool autumn breeze danced through the house, bringing with it all of the scents of the farm.

"Once you've lived in the country, the smells will remain in your memory forever," Lila told me.

Fall's incredible beauty was transforming the farm. The night air, once warm and humid, had been replaced with a fresh, cool crispness. I could see my breath every time I spoke, and with the pond now too cold to rest my feet in, it became obvious our days of splashing in the sun would soon be ending. However, Hunner and I made sure to make the most out of our remaining time. We lay along the edge of the pond in the tall grasses, soaking in the warmth of the sun and basking in the beauty of all the deep colors of trees. Nature showered upon us a spiritual bathing. Cottonwoods laced the pond, and their leaves shimmered as the breeze gently rocked the branches back and forth. The dance of the leaves and the twinkling of light enthralled me, and I felt as if I were absent from the physical world. The tall grass gently brushed across my face, every so often waking me from the dream I had fallen into.

With each hour and day that passed, as the sun rose and fell, Lila continued to harvest crops. She was busier than any one woman should be, with little time left for herself. She was lost in the daily duties of the farm, and she had long since stopped paying attention to her own needs. Everything on the farm was going through a change, a metamorphosis of sorts, as winter slowly crept over the land. Nature began to softly close its eyes for the long night ahead, with the expectation of a new birth and awakening to be brought forth in the spring. All would soon settle down for a cold winter on the farm.

I often wondered how things were settling in for Gabe. Prison might have slowed him down for the time being, but it was only temporary, and once he had his freedom, he would quickly regain his reign on the streets. I had been on the farm for a little over a month, and I missed him, especially at night when I thought about the two of us sleeping under the stars. I felt guilty knowing that he was sleeping with one eye open in prison while I was sleeping comfortably in my mother's bed.

One evening while left alone, I combed the house searching for stationery, an envelope, and some stamps. Successful in my attempt, I spent an entire night writing Gabe a five-page letter. I poured my heart onto the paper, pleading for him to come for me as soon as he was released from prison. I included specific details, including the address of the farm and Lila's schedule. Should he come for me, I wanted to avoid any confrontation between the two of them.

Early one morning, Hunner and I walked to the end of the long road. I stood staring at the mailbox for several minutes before placing the letter inside. I was sure Lila wouldn't approve of me writing to him, and it wasn't worth the risk of asking permission. Although the farm was comfortable and Lila's efforts were inviting, I didn't belong here. If she really knew who I was, she would know that too. I felt Mom everywhere, and I still had questions about why she would leave. I hoped to have that conversation with Lila before I left.

Entering the kitchen, I made sure to open the door slowly. Just like the porch door, it screeched and sent shivers up my spine. Lila grumbled to herself every time she heard the annoying sound and made a note that it was one more thing she needed to fix. "I gotta get that fixed" was quickly becoming the farm motto.

"Hurry, Sophie!" Lila shouted, as I peeked through the kitchen door. "Robert is coming up the drive. Go ask him to join us for breakfast."

"Seriously, it's freezing out there, and I don't have my shoes on yet," I replied sharply.

"Go, go! You'll miss him if you don't hurry." She started shooing me out the door.

With no shoes on, I flew off the back porch to flag Robert down on his tractor. I waved my arms back and forth and jumped up and down, looking as if I had gone mad. When he finally noticed me, he pulled the tractor over and jumped quickly from the cab. Approaching me, he slapped his pant leg with his hat to shake the dust off. A cloud of dust encompassed him.

"Is everything all right?" he asked, with a look of concern.

"Oh yes, everything's okay," I replied, as my face turned six sheets of red with embarrassment.

"Well, you had me scared there for a minute," he said, with a kind smile. "You were jumping around like the house was on fire or you had red ants in your shorts." He laughed. "So you must be Sophie." He reached out to shake my hand.

"The one and only," I replied, smiling back at him. He put me at ease with his humor and honest smile. "Lila wanted me to ask you to join us for breakfast."

"Well, Sophie, if you've eaten Lila's pancakes, then you know that's an offer I can't refuse," he said gratefully. We walked back toward the house in anticipation of Lila's breakfast feast.

Robert's smile accompanied his air of authenticity. I didn't have to wonder why Lila liked and trusted him so much.

Upon entering the house, he turned to me. Leaning into my ear, he whispered, "I'm glad you're here, Sophie. Ms. Lila really needs you. And I'll bet you need her too. She's a good woman. Be easy on her." He smiled. "Besides, there's a reason you're here. I'm not even sure that I know what it is. Just give God time, and he'll show the both of you."

Stepping into the kitchen, Robert paused for a moment and looked at both Lila and me. Something had surely tickled his funny bone because he began to laugh to himself. We stood dumbfounded, wondering what was so funny.

"Well, if I hadn't seen it myself, I wouldn't have believed it," he said, chuckling.

"What?" Lila said with a taste of anger on her tongue as we both waited for Robert to reveal what he found so amusing about the two of us.

"Well, I don't think I've ever seen a beautiful young lady look so much like her grandmother. I'll let you two decide who gets the compliment." He pulled a chair from the table to sit down.

"Aren't you the comedian this morning," Lila said as she turned to continue with breakfast. "You may have me rethinking my offer if you don't behave." She grinned.

Robert spent many long days and evenings well into the darkness, helping Lila bring the crops in from the fields before winter set in. He was a tall, well-built man, his skin roughened by the sun. His graying hair looked good on him. He didn't appear old, just distinguished. Lila said he reminded her of Andy Griffith from television. His smile was captivating and, along with his fun-loving character, made you feel welcome in his presence. Lila said he loved to tell jokes, but he never got the punch line right. However, he was always quick to laugh at himself, which made it even more pleasant to be in his company.

Breakfast this morning was interesting as Robert shared his love for the farm. "God blessed me with rich land," he said. "Working on the land is working for God. He gives me the strength and all the tools I need, and I offer him a bountiful harvest." He stated all this with sincere conviction.

"You make it sound so easy," I replied.

"Well, Sophie, it's been anything but easy," Robert declared. "Even with all the pleasure I find in the land, there have been times that have tested my belief and brought me to my knees. Twice, tornadoes destroyed my farm, killing most of my livestock and ripping the crops right out of the ground."

"I'm sorry," I said, feeling a bit guilty. I had assumed farm life was easy.

"You don't need to be sorry, Sophie. It's in the midst of hardship that we learn our greatest lessons. I never questioned what I needed to do next. I rebuilt my farm as if God was watching, and he has blessed me far beyond my own expectations."

Robert shared breakfast with Lila and me over the next few weeks while they worked day and night harvesting the crops. I had never met a man of such great character and integrity. Robert Taylor was a new and refreshing symbol of what God meant for all men to be. Over time, I realized he was consistent in his faith and would offer a helping hand to anyone in need, regardless of who they were or what their situation. Robert said character is who we are when no one else is looking. Being around him made me want to be a better person, and I understood why Lila treasured her friendship with Robert and Hilly.

I hadn't met Hilly yet, but if she was anything like Lila had described, I knew I would like her too. Lila said she was the best baker in Morton Falls, and her cakes won first place many times at the county fair. Lila assured me that she would ask Hilly to make me a cake for my upcoming birthday. I suggested red velvet cake; it was my favorite.

Days passed quickly on the farm. Mid-November became increasingly cool, and the leaves fallen from the trees formed a thick carpet covering the ground with the warmest colors of orange and gold. I settled into the daily routine of the farm, with Lila allowing me the space I needed to grow into my new surroundings. We were respectful of each other, and I tried to help her as much as possible.

I began to see more of myself in Lila and more of her in me. I knew now more than ever that we were cut from the same cloth. We even had some of the same habits. We both scraped crumbs from around our plate, sweeping them off the side of the table into our hands and shaking them back onto our food. I had done it for a lifetime, never thinking that something so trivial rested in my DNA. Neither of us graceful, we laughed at one another when one of us tripped. We didn't always need to talk. Sometimes, we could be silent, and we seemed to read each other's minds.

Hunner was my constant companion, and although his snoring bothered me, he became my best friend and my foot warmer at night. Lila often warned me to keep Hunner off the bed. Well, that was my and Hunner's little secret, just one of many.

Lila was careful to make sure she followed precisely the court order the judge had set forth, which meant enrolling me in high school. The school nearest the farm was about a five-mile drive and situated in the small farming town of Saint Paul. The school was smaller than what I had been accustomed to in River Crossing, and walking in halfway through the second quarter left an uneasy feeling in my stomach.

"You're a survivor, Sophie," Lila stated supportively. "You'll be all right."

"I know how to take care of myself," I replied with a sneer.

"I know it's going to be awkward at first, but I'm sure you'll fit in just fine. Hilly was at the bake sale after church last week, and she told me many of the kids were asking about you."

"They need to mind their own business," I replied with attitude.

I had gotten comfortable on the farm without any disturbances, and the idea of going back to school seemed somewhat childish after the life I had experienced.

"I know it's not going to be easy for you after everything you've been through, but an education is a privilege, and I believe you deserve that," Lila said, as if she were offering me a gift.

Lila was fierce in her belief that everyone deserved and needed a good education. Her encouragement and strong will helped me to accept and prepare for school. I felt like a little child entering kindergarten again. I was scared, but at the same time excited, knowing that I would be attending the same school my mother graduated from. The history of her presence there in some way made me feel more comfortable.

Although I had missed most of my junior year, and the senior year was slipping away, Lila convinced the school principal to allow me to join class as a senior with peers of my own age. While she was successful in her persuasion, the result came with strings attached. Lila gave me an account of her talk with Mr. Harter.

"Mrs. Randolph, Sophie has missed almost a year and a half of school, and you expect me to overlook this?" Mr. Harter said.

Lila pleaded with him. "I understand, Mr. Harter, and I fully recognize your position, but I'm asking you to look at Sophie's credits and grades before...well, before her mother's death. She was an excellent student, and I believe she has every right to be given a chance to prove herself and enter a classroom with young adults of her age."

"I can't just let her waltz back into class without some sort of an attempt to rectify the time she has missed," he said. He rubbed his head in frustration, searching for a resolution.

"I know the position I'm putting you in, and whatever the decision, I promise you, I will be grateful for your consideration." Lila ended her plea and picked up her purse to exit his office. "Thank you, Mr. Harter."

"Wait a minute, wait a minute!" Mr. Harter called, sounding irritated. "She is to begin school immediately with a full schedule, no study halls, and with completion of summer school, I will allow her to graduate with her class...as long as there's no trouble."

"I promise you there will be no trouble," Lila said, giving her word. "Thank you so much for your kindness and consideration, Mr. Harter. It won't go unnoticed at the next board meeting." She smiled.

Lila and I had grown to live peacefully under the same roof, both of us careful to not cross each other's boundaries. Although we were still very quiet with one another, each day, I grew more and more certain that she had my back. She had promised Mr. Harter there would be no trouble. I, on the other hand, wasn't so sure. Nonetheless, I would give it a shot.

Starting over was beginning to feel good. Shortly after Mom died, nothing mattered, especially school. She believed as Lila did, that a good education was not only a necessary and critical step for personal growth, but for the welfare of our country, which needs good and decent law-abiding citizens. With Lila's help, I was able to begin picking up the pieces of the past and start putting back together a life that I had once loved. I developed new perspectives each day, and I could breathe easier and lighter as the weights of hell were slowly diminishing.

However, the memories of the past year were much harder to rid myself of, as they were laced with shame and humiliation. I would never be able to relieve my mind of the fear that encapsulated every part of my body while being raped. You have to put some things in a box, close the lid, find a closet in your mind for the box, and then shut the door and lock it securely. It was my secret, and only I held the key.

With a five-mile drive to Saint Paul, I begged Lila to let me drive Old Blue to school. "Only idiots ride the bus," I said, pleading my case.

"You will take the bus," she said firmly.

"I know how to drive a stick, and I'm damn good at it," I argued.

"Sophie, you will take the bus, just like the other students," Lila stated sternly. "And please watch your language."

"Don't you trust me?" I asked in an attempt to arouse feelings of guilt.

"It isn't a question of trust," Lila replied. "I'm very busy, and I don't have time to argue all day. This topic is no longer up for discussion."

I stomped to my room in defeat. She could be a tough cookie at times, just like me.

The first day of walking onto the bus was exactly what I had expected—awkward. I was welcomed with cold, hard stares. Pretending not to notice, I rode looking out the window.

Whispers back and forth between the girls proved more annoying than they were uncomfortable. A few seats in front of me, two girls wearing cheerleading uniforms began giggling and talking about me as if I didn't notice. Or maybe they were brave enough to think that I wouldn't kick their asses when the bus stopped.

"I heard she's an orphan," one quipped.

"She looks like a slut," the other girl retorted. She giggled as her ponytail flipped back and forth.

"I heard she was in prison," whispered another.

As the bus came to a stop in front of the school, I was fully aware of what lay ahead of me. I was living in Peyton Place. The bus driver opened the doors, and everyone quickly scrambled off the bus. When my feet hit the ground, my eyes fell upon a large two-story red brick school building. A statue of a woman reading a book adorned the entrance with an inscription that read, "For my eyes lay on these pages; my mind is filled with dreams."

Quickly catching up to the two giddy cheerleaders who had so rudely insulted my character, I gently tapped them both on the shoulder. When they turned in surprise, I greeted them. "Hi." I smiled, simulating their extreme enthusiasm. I flippantly swung my hair from side to side. "Remember me?"

With puckered brows, they scowled, looking at me as if I were an object of disgust.

"I'm the new girl on the bus," I said, leaning in closer to whisper. "You're right, I was in prison. Please don't tell anyone. Most people frown on murder." Walking away, I laughed to myself. I looked back, and noticing I had knocked the bobby socks right off their feet, I was pleased. The expression on their faces was priceless.

Entering the school office, I was welcomed enthusiastically by the office staff.

"You must be Lila's granddaughter," an older woman said as she approached me, smiling from ear to ear. Greeting me as if I were a long-lost relative, she was surely eager to help. "I have your class schedule right here, and I'll show you to your locker. We're so excited to have you. Any relative of Lila's is a friend of mine."

"Thank you, ma'am," I said.

The locker next to mine belonged to a very good-looking young man. He welcomed me with a warm smile.

"Sophie, if you need anything, just come to the office," the woman accompanying me said. "My name is Betty, but the students call me Mrs. Butcher. I know, I know. It's my married name." She chuckled and proceeded back to the office. With her cheerful face, plump rosy cheeks, and hair as white as snow, she reminded me of Mrs. Claus from one of my Christmas books I had when I was a child. She certainly didn't look like a Mrs. Butcher.

"Is that really her name?" I asked the young man standing next to my locker.

"That's really her name," he replied, still smiling. His smile was infectious—and perfect. He put his hand out to shake mine. "Hi. My name's Blake." His voice was soft.

I stood for a moment, feeling a bit clumsy. His handshake was strong, and I felt like a moth being drawn to a flame. "Hi. I'm Sophie." My voice rattled, mimicking Lila's shaky voice.

Our handshake was abruptly interrupted by the ringing of the bell.

"Let me see your schedule," he said. "I'll show you to your first class. Hurry."

Running swiftly through the halls, Blake accompanied me to the appropriate room. His act of kindness and friendly smile gave me a warm welcome.

Saint Paul High School was established in 1922. The building was old as well as the classrooms. Chalkboards were worn, with the thousands of sweeps across them showing their age. Desks were engraved with interesting markings of students past. I hoped to find an engraving from my mother and looked forward to switching seats every day.

All of the teachers were friendly, and each one talked of Lila and how much they admired her. I hadn't realized her position in the community, but she was becoming as important to me as I could see she was to others. Her heart certainly extended beyond the farm. Many of the teachers who remember my mother spoke fondly of her and bragged about her amazing artistic abilities. I withdrew immediately from any conversation regarding her, as it was still too painful.

Classroom sizes were smaller than what I had been used to in River Crossing. On average, there were seven to ten students per class, and not one of them acted like a big happy family, as Lila—when I first arrived here—had indicated everyone in River Crossing did.

I managed to find every class, and at the end of the day, Blake and I met again as we unloaded books into our lockers.

"How was your first day?" he asked.

"I survived."

"It'll get better. I promise."

"Thanks. And thanks for helping me find my class this morning."

"Did you ride the bus?" he asked as he stuffed his last book into his locker.

"Unfortunately," I replied.

"That'll get better, too." He laughed. "Where are you staying?"

"The Randolph farm." I said it quietly, hoping no one else could hear.

"I know that farm. Maybe sometime we could..."

"I gotta go!" I yelled before he could get the words out. "I'm sure they won't wait for me. Thanks again."

The bus ride home was far more comfortable than the morning ride. The two cheerleaders sat as far away from me as they possibly could, every so often looking to make sure I was a safe distance away.

The bus dropped me off at the end of our long driveway, and upon hearing my footsteps scrambling up the road, Hunner quickly welcomed me home.

Lila waited on the porch in anticipation. Smiling her famous half smile, she clapped her hands together when she saw me nearing. "It was okay, right?" she asked eagerly, her hands crossed and placed over her heart.

"I'd rather castrate pigs," I said with a sour taste in my mouth.

Lila's smile quickly vanished, and her hands fell to her side in disappointment. "Well, that can be arranged, I guess," she said shortly, retreating into the house.

School continued to be tolerable, and I kept my promise to Lila by delivering good grades and keeping out of trouble. I even excelled in a writing class, with honorable mentions for my poetry and short stories. It wasn't surprising that I was well received by the boys at school. I knew how to draw them in like flies, and they followed me as if I had put a spell on them. However, I kept mostly to myself; it was safer that way. The girls were distant and unfriendly, exactly how I liked them. I especially enjoyed provoking Penelope and Tiffany, the two perky cheerleaders who hung tight to Blake as if to protect him from me.

Blake's locker being positioned right beside mine allowed for brief small talk throughout the day. His friendliness took me by surprise, and his kindness was something that I hadn't been a witness to in a young man. I began comparing notes in my head, questioning my relationship with Gabe.

I looked forward to the end of the day when I got on the bus and drifted into thought as I peered out the window awaiting my arrival back to the place that had saved me, the farm.

Chapter 5

The evenings of sitting on the porch had ended. Instead, Lila, Hunner, and I stayed in front of the fireplace keeping warm with a delicious cup of hot chocolate. Cursing the cold, Lila sat in her chair and rubbed lotion on her dry cracked hands and feet. Chores on the farm never ceased, and the cold Nebraska weather was brutal to the body. It made a person wonder if they were crazy to stay year after year on the farm.

Just when I thought things were perfect, Lila suggested I accompany her to the Sunday church service. Up to now, I had enjoyed spending my Sunday mornings with Hunner. We were both living the life of a dog, lazy and happy, exactly the way we liked it. I wanted nothing to do with God or his church. In fact, I was certain I could live without him and the hypocrites that feed upon him like vultures. I had found comfort on the farm and peace in nature that filled my soul.

Lila was fierce in her belief, yet she spoke kindly. "Sophie, I know how you feel. There was a time in my life that I cursed the Lord just as you're doing now. I turned my back on him as if he were the reason for every wrongdoing that had ever been done to me. Finally, I realized that even though I had turned away from him, he had never left me. He had always been there, waiting with an undeniable and unconditional love that I had never known before. I know it's hard for you to understand with everything you've been through, but I promise you this: he has never left you."

"You have no idea what I've been through!" I shouted defiantly. "Was he there when your daughter left you? Because he wasn't there when he took her from me. You have no right to assume you know what I've experienced. And you think you're gonna fix it all with a God who has screwed both of us."

"You're right, Sophie," Lila said slowly. "I apologize. I shouldn't assume I know what you've been through."

I stood motionless, my anger slowly dissipating after her apology. Lila began to cry, and this was the first time I seen her react with such emotion. Tears poured from her eyes, rolling down her cheeks and falling upon her breasts. My words had ripped through her heart. Though I had had every intention of hurting her, I also knew I had gone too far, and my heart became heavy with each tear that fell. Now I stood before her ashamed and awkwardly unaware of what to do or what to say.

In defeat, she lifted her apron, wiped away her tears, and sighed. Silence fell upon us, and Lila retreated quietly to the kitchen.

I stood by the staircase in the foyer, looking out onto the land, overcome with a feeling of disgrace. "I'll go!" I yelled reluctantly. "But don't expect miracles."

Lila came running through the kitchen door, trying not to act too excited. That proved nearly impossible, as beams of joy emanated from her entire body.

But I knew it would take a lot more than church to bring me close to God. It would truly take a miracle.

Lila ascended the stairs and came back down again faster than usual, eager to present me with a dress she had bought just for this occasion. How did she know I would go? I was beginning to think she was far smarter than I was willing to give her credit for. I loved the dress. I hadn't worn anything so beautiful since Mom's funeral. Unwilling to share my pleasure, I grabbed it from her and retreated to my room.

I couldn't wait to try it on and quickly pulled it over my head and down over my body. It fit me like a glove. The color of cream and embellished with shiny pearls, the dress appeared rich as silk. Roses embroidered around the neck and down the sleeves gave me a delicate air of sophistication.

I stood looking at myself in the mirror and began to reflect back to when Mom and I would dress up and go to church together. Often, we would joke about which one of us was prettier. She always said I won hands down, but at this moment, looking in the mirror, I saw her in me, and we both won.

I rode beside Lila in Old Blue to church on the next Sunday morning. Enjoying the brisk, cool breeze and listening to the birds singing, I felt intensely in tune with nature. As we drove down the old roads, I could see the bare branches blowing in the wind as if they were moving to the music I was hearing in my mind. The sky was the bluest I had ever seen, and only a few clouds rested gently on its canvas. A bird flew from a fence post, and I imagined myself flying beside it. Every sound outside the truck was clear, as if it were made by an orchestra playing inside my head. I had never in my life been this connected to my natural surroundings. The farm seemed to have a power of its own, sneaking up on me without warning. Once captured, I was in awe of its wonder.

Lila parked Old Blue at the edge of the parking lot, and we got out and headed to the church. I reluctantly followed a step behind her, hoping not to be noticed. I wanted to sit in the pew closest to the door, just in case I needed to make a quick escape, but Lila proceeded directly to the front. Just as I had imagined, as we walked forward, every eye in the church was on us. It seemed to me that the entire congregation stared us down from head to foot. It felt like we were uninvited guests crashing a party. *Maybe God should send out invitations*, I thought to myself.

As we approached our seats, I noticed a familiar face from school staring at me. "What?" I mouthed with a scowl. He quickly turned his head in the other direction. Lila gave him her famous closed-lip half smile, though he wasn't looking, and we took our seats.

After settling in beside Lila, I glanced across the aisle. Blake Gerard was now staring straight ahead with marked determination. I stifled a giggle and turned my attention to the minister.

Moments later, I felt Blake's eyes on me again. I turned my head and caught him in the act, only this time I smiled. When Blake smiled back, I felt my face redden. I quickly snapped my head back toward the altar.

In my opinion, and in the opinion of most of the girls at school, Blake was the cutest boy in the class. He had big brown eyes, wavy dark-brown hair, and a little dimple on his right cheek. His smile on my first day at school as he stood beside my locker had made me feel just a little less crazy.

His smile a moment ago had sent my heart pounding. The more I tried to focus on the minister's message, the less I was able to do so. It was taking everything I had to keep from looking back at Blake. I took a deep breath and tried to calm myself. Lila must have picked up on my tension because she reached down and patted my knee. She probably thought I was still nervous about attending church. Little did she know, church was the last thing on my mind.

Not surprisingly, Blake was one of the most popular boys at school. With his good looks, perfect grades, and personality—kind and friendly to everyone—he was admired by students and teachers alike. These were only a few of his assets, not to mention his ass! My stomach lurched. Why was the amazing Blake Gerard staring at *me*?

Unable to resist any longer, I allowed my eyes to drift across the aisle. There he was, still staring, a great big smile lighting up his face. Again, I smiled back. I realized that, for the first time since starting school, I wasn't dreading Monday morning.

I ignored the sermon, just as I had planned. I couldn't stop flirting with Blake. My small seductive smiles were obvious, accompanied with a flutter of the eyelashes, a gentle turn of the head, and a lowering of the eyes. He had been bewitched by my charm, and I, by his.

An unbidden memory pulled me back to reality. My mind drifted back to a fateful night in Lincoln. Gabe had taken my hand and squeezed it tightly as we entered the gas station, assuring me he wouldn't let anything happen to me. I trembled in fear as he held the gun to the attendant's head and sent me around the checkout counter to collect money from the cash register.

"Get the money, you idiot!" he screamed. "You screw this up, I'll kill you."

"I'm sorry, I'm so sorry," I whispered to the clerk, who was removing money from the register. Shaking hysterically, with fear running through every vein of my body, I began crying uncontrollably and begged Gabe to stop.

"Get the money!" he yelled.

Panic consumed me. The sound of his voice, the horror of his threats—I found myself frozen in fear. Gabe didn't plan the things that could go wrong that day, but there were many, including the presence of a police officer. As the officer exited the restroom, Gabe spotted him and ran. I was left standing with the officer's service revolver pointed at my forehead. For a moment, I sadly hoped he would pull the trigger. I was ready for death, and I wanted to see my mother. Nothing on earth could compete with what was waiting for me, and life was far more threatening than death.

I had replayed this event in my mind a thousand times, and I still wondered why the officer spared my life. Gabe was apprehended a few days later and sentenced to the correctional facility in Lincoln, Nebraska.

After a long hour on a hard bench at church, my ass was numb and my mind paralyzed. But something good always comes from sacrifice; the good minister assured us all that we were saved. Hallelujah!

As we approached Old Blue in the parking lot, it was evident that there were a few old bags snubbing Lila. *Or are they snubbing me?* I wondered. They whispered among themselves, with the palms of their hands covering their mouths, and peered noticeably at us.

"Don't look at them, Sophie," Lila said sternly. "Just keep walking and don't stare."

Lila quickly exited the church parking lot. Driving by the church ladies, she acted as if she hadn't noticed their gawking. She was silent, but the expression on her face spoke for her. She looked as if she could turn around and run them over with Old Blue without blinking an eye. Wow! What had happened to kind, gentle, sweet Lila? All of a sudden, she reminded me of me. I was now more convinced than ever that we had the same DNA. I liked this side of her.

As we sped down the old dirt road, curiosity got the better of me. And if curiosity could kill a cat, well, it shot the hell out of me. I wanted to know everything. "Who are those old bats?" I asked excitedly.

"No one you need to be concerned with, Sophie," Lila replied sharply.

"Are you kidding me? They were totally rude."

"It's not our place to judge."

"Well, pardon me, but it surely looked like we were the ones being judged."

"It has nothing to do with you, Sophie, I can assure you," Lila said bitterly. "They're just women with too much time on their hands."

"Do you know them?"

"All too well." She scoffed. "Vivian Gerard, Lou Lou Bell Roberts, and Beatrice Meyer."

I was dying to know more, but I could tell from the look on Lila's face that it wasn't going to be today.

"Sophie," she said, confirming my thoughts, "this story is for another day."

I was disappointed, but somehow, I knew that eventually this mystery, too, would unravel itself. I couldn't wait to hear the story. I was certain it would be worth every juicy detail.

Chapter 6

Winter had set in, and typical of Nebraska weather, the bitter cold chilled us to the bone and all but kept us inside. With the ground now covered with shimmering icy-cold snow, it looked as if a million diamonds had blanketed the earth. In the sun, it nearly blinded us. Outside of feeding the animals and robbing hens of their eggs, Lila, Hunner, and I retreated to the farmhouse.

"This is the time to stop and reflect as the year is coming to an end," Lila said. "God intends for all of us to rest and appreciate the beauty he has bestowed upon us: the incredible awakening in spring as the flowers begin creeping up through the green tender strands of grass, the summer sun's warmth on our bodies at the lake, and the delicious colors that surround us in the fall. As we sit in the company of each other and the year closes, we should reflect on another year that God has blessed us with the joy of life and the gift of love. Those are the most important things there are.

"Sophie, I know you're still struggling, trying to find your way, and I do apologize if I sound like a preacher. I wish there were a way I could ease the pain, but I know I can't. Life comes with lots of lessons, and nobody leaves this world unscathed. But you come from a line of strong women. We may get knocked down, but we get back up and wipe the sand from our feet, and we keep going."

As I sat listening to Lila preach about God and everything he had blessed me with, I was reminded of my mother. I was sure

I had heard that exact speech from her years earlier. Something was slowly changing inside of me. With every word Lila spoke, she was teaching me, and every moment I was in her presence, I was growing. I was beginning to like her. She loved me without condition, and love, simply stated, was bringing me back to life. It's incredible to be loved, and when it comes in its purest form, it changes everything.

"Tell me about your parents," I said curiously.

"I thought you'd never ask."

It was obvious Lila had been waiting for this moment. Up to now, we hadn't spoken much of my mother or her family. I could see the excitement on Lila's face as she placed pillows behind her back to get comfortable in her chair. I perched myself up against the sofa, and Hunner slept in front of the fireplace. The chilly winter night with the smell of the wood burning and the crackling noise from the fireplace provided the perfect setting for me to hear Lila's story.

"Well, Sophie, I was a nineteen-year-old spirited young lady when I came to Morton Falls. The year was 1956. My daddy said I was an angel with a lot of attitude. If someone were to ask me about you, I believe that's how I would describe you too." She laughed. "I was born in Pilsner, Czechoslovakia. When I was four, my parents moved us to the incredible shores of America—New York City." When she spoke of her birthplace and her parents, her voice took on a bit of an accent. "My parents were immigrants from Czechoslovakia. My father's name was Loren Rasmussen, and my mother's name was Olive. You also remind me a lot of my mother." She smiled. "You both have incredible survivor instincts. Her bravery, as well as that of my father, outshines anything that I have ever done in my life. I'd like to take credit for having even an inkling of her strength.

"My father's oldest brother, Will, had come to America a few years earlier. He wrote my father, describing its beauty and the promise of prosperity in exchange for an honest man's hard work.

Even though it was incredibly difficult for both of my parents, they left their friends and family and the comfort of all they had ever known to come to America with the hope of one thing: to give me a better life. They were people of simple means and never asked anything for themselves. Their sacrifice was entirely for me. Their unselfishness is unmatched." Lila bowed her head in thought as she reminisced about her parents and the long-ago past.

I sat quietly, lost in my own thoughts.

Lila lifted her head and began speaking again. "My mother was a talented seamstress, and there wasn't anything she couldn't make with a little material and a needle and thread. In those days, you didn't go shopping for a dress, you went shopping for a pattern. It was a special time for me and my mother when she let me pick out my own McCall's pattern. Everything I wore was made by my mother's hands, and she made sure everything I wore was beautiful. Thinking back now, it makes me appreciate her even more. These memories bring such joy to my heart."

"Your mother sounds a lot like mine," I commented. "My mother loved to make beautiful dresses for me and my dolls."

"Well, she certainly had a great teacher." Lila smiled. "Your mother spent a few weeks every summer in New York, and my mother taught her everything she knew about sewing. Grace loved it as much as my mother. Grace loved the time she spent with both her grandparents. My father used to call her his little dumpling. She adored sitting on his lap while he sang songs to her from his homeland."

"I wish she would have told me about them," I said, feeling a sense of loss at having missed out on a part of my mother's life.

"I know, Sophie," Lila said with an air of sadness in her voice. "And I wish they could have seen you. They died within months of each other shortly after you were born. I knew one couldn't live without the other. My mother passed away from cancer, and my father passed away eight months later—for no reason; he just died in his sleep. He was a strong man, but if there was one thing he couldn't live without, it was the love of his life."

"I totally get that," I replied, knowing how empty I felt at the loss of my mother.

"My father and I were very close," Lila continued. "He was a strong man and firm in what he stood for. You didn't have to guess where you stood with him. You're like that yourself, Sophie. I like that about you." She paused. "He had always dreamed of opening his own specialty meat store, and after several years of long hours and hard work, his dream—the American dream—came to life. His store was small, but his accomplishment was huge, and he was a man of great pride. I can still taste his homemade sausage and cured ham. Just thinking about them makes me hungry." She laughed. "I was blessed with more love than most people get in a lifetime."

Hearing Lila talk about her father made me feel, for the first time in my life, like I had missed out on something. I didn't know who my father was and had never really wanted to know... until now.

"I loved growing up in New York," Lila continued. "It's magical, with city streetlights that stretch as far as the eye can see. There's an incredible energy in the city that can't be described, you have to experience it." She stood up. "All this talk of food and New York City has made me hungry."

Lila and I retreated to the kitchen for a snack and closed the evening with full bellies and the beginning of a newfound friendship.

Winter was a perfect time for baking as the ovens kept the kitchen warm. It was a great place to retreat for conversation and hot tea to warm the body. Conversation was becoming more inviting, and I was learning more about Lila than I thought I would ever care to learn.

"I dreamed one day of opening my own bakery," she said matter-of-factly at the kitchen table. "If I didn't have to tend to the farm, that's what I would do with my time, that's really where my heart is."

"I think that would be great," I said, my voice muffled by a mouth full of pancakes.

"It probably wouldn't be very successful. We'd eat all the profits!" She laughed.

She was right. I had already gained a few much-needed pounds since I had been on the farm. Particles of pancakes flew from my mouth as I snickered. Together, we found ourselves quite amusing.

Lila loved baking, and everything she created in the kitchen was food for the soul. I had never eaten a chocolate cake that could come close to hers. The smell was divine, the taste was indescribable, and each bite melted in my mouth like butter. She often said the secret was in the eggs, but I'm sure she said that to throw everyone off. Whatever the real secret, she didn't share it with anyone. You would've thought she had invented the chocolate egg or something, the way she talked.

I loved to watch Lila cook. She hummed religious ballads as she moved throughout the kitchen carefully checking items in the oven. Each time she opened the oven door, her eyes lit up as if there were a present waiting for her inside. She was certainly in her element, and I could see how much she loved it. But her greatest joy was sharing what she had made with others. She took each compliment as if it were an award.

As Lila moved around the kitchen, I sat by the window, entranced, and peered through the frost-laden glass. I watched the squirrels as they ran up and down and about the oak trees, the sound of the leaves blowing in the wind, and the smell of the cattle in the fields. The frogs belting out at the pond were all gone and forgotten, but a new rebirth was taking place. Outside, the cold was extreme, but the ice on the trees, the glistening snow, and everything white seemed so clean and pure. The dead oak trees that still stood around the farm were covered with a frosting

Chapter 7

My seventeenth birthday was only a few days away, and Lila became quite embarrassing, making such a stink about it to everyone. I felt very uncomfortable with all the attention.

"Hilly is going to make your favorite cake, red velvet, for your birthday," Lila said excitedly. "I wanted to make your cake myself, but if you know Hilly, it isn't worth the battle. She always wins." Lila grunted.

"It's okay," I replied.

"I guess I should have asked if it was all right to invite some friends over for your birthday," Lila said, questioning her lack of concern for my wishes. "We can do something different if you want. We could just go shopping or to dinner or a movie. Any suggestions?"

"No, really, it's okay,"

"Would you like to invite some of your friends from school?"

"Seriously?" I replied condescendingly. "I have to spend all day with those idiots. I don't think so."

Lila was trying hard to make me feel comfortable, sometimes too hard. In fact, it had the opposite effect. The harder she tried, the more uncomfortable I felt. We were still working on boundaries with one another, and there were times of push and shove. But for the most part, we had made progress, yet held a distance between our pasts.

of snow, transforming them into statues of beauty. I sat th
often wished I could be transformed as they were. Alt
didn't know it at the time, I was.

fr
of
yo
A

wit

too
trie
bou
sho
safe

My birthday arrived, and it was just as I had expected: Robert told bad jokes, and Hilly talked about what she would be baking for the Christmas raffle. Hilly also had a passion for baking, as if it were the very thread that kept her breathing. She was what I pictured a grandma would look like—short, with the many years of cupcakes and cookies attached to her hips; graying hair; and a loveable smile. Her personality was bubbly, and even when no one else laughed at Robert's terrible jokes, she did. There was a great love between the Taylors, and I wondered if Lila and my grandfather had shared the same. Lila decorated the entire house with streamers and balloons, and just as she had promised, Hilly prepared a delicious red velvet cake.

"Eat some more cake!" Hilly shouted at me while slicing up another piece.

"I've had three pieces," I replied, holding my stomach. "I couldn't squeeze in another one if I tried." The mere thought of more cake made me feel sick.

"You're nothing but skin and bones," she sputtered. "Lila, have you been feeding this child?"

Lila and I looked at each other and smiled.

"No, I keep her locked up in the cellar, and she only gets enough bread and water to keep her alive," Lila said jokingly.

"Well, that's what it looks like," Hilly shot back with a scowl.

"Leave the girl alone," Robert admonished Hilly. "She looks just fine."

"Thank you," I mouthed to Robert. I remained silent for fear that Hilly would whisk me away and shove red velvet cake down my throat until I looked like her.

"There ain't nothing wrong with a little meat on the bones," Hilly crowed.

You're right, but you took all the meat, I thought, laughing to myself.

My seventeenth birthday surely wasn't what I would have expected. Peers my own age might have thought it quite boring, but to me, it felt like I had a real family. I laughed at horrible jokes and stuffed myself with red velvet cake that was beyond my wildest dreams, and the best was yet to come—my present. My passion for writing was developing as strongly as Hilly's passion for baking. Lila was excited that I had found something that inspired me, and she believed God had given me an incredible gift, the gift of words. She loved to sit at night on the porch and read the poems I had written, and she got pleasure from bragging to friends and neighbors about her talented granddaughter. It made me feel good.

Lila couldn't contain her excitement. Smiling ear to ear, she handed me a small box, beautifully wrapped. I opened it slowly, wanting to savor every moment. Inside, a lovely pen set was inscribed, *Let your heart be your guide. Let the words flow through it. With love, Lila.*

It was the greatest gift I had ever received.

Falling into bed that evening, I began to praise and thank God for all he had given me. I no longer cursed him for what I thought he had taken. I now longed to hear Rosco crow in the morning, and every bit of the farm felt like a romance. I couldn't help but fall in love.

Chapter 8

Christmas arrived, and Lila and I cut a tree north of the farm and carried it back to the house. We laughed as snow fell from the tree upon our heads with each step we took. Lila brought out several boxes of ornaments and decorations that she had collected over the years and had stored in a chest. Each box was marked with a name, a year, or both, and as we hung them carefully on the tree, Lila shared the sentiment attached to each of the items. Two boxes remained on the floor beside her chair.

"Take a look in this box, Sophie." Lila smiled with delight as she handed me one of the boxes.

"My name's on this box," I said with surprise. The box appeared old, yet my name could clearly be seen through the dust.

"I purchased an ornament every year, just for you," Lila said softly.

Smiling, she lovingly watched me as I cautiously removed the first ornament from the box. Overcome with emotion, I read the words, *Baby's First Christmas*. I couldn't believe that after all these years, Lila hadn't forgotten me or given up on the thought that she would ever see me again. I realized she was an incredible woman of faith, perseverance, and especially, hope.

As I unwrapped each ornament, she recited exactly when and where she had purchased it. It was as if she had made each purchase with the hope that one day we would be together right here, in this time, hanging each item with precise placement on the tree as if we were building an exquisite piece of art.

I lowered my head in thought.

She placed her hand lightly on my back. "Sophie," she said with a soft smile, "I never forgot you. I couldn't forget you. You were an angel."

Tears welled up in my eyes, and Lila helped put the last ornament in place. Wiping my eyes, I gazed at the glistening tree. We stood in silence and stared as if we had both been hypnotized by its beauty. I wanted this moment engraved in my memory forever. Lila had waited so long for this day to happen. Her patience was unimaginable, and love emanated from the pores of her skin. I hoped one day I could be half as patient and gracious as she.

Hunner lay warming himself by the fire as Lila rocked gently, admiring the tree.

"There's another box beside your rocker," I said, drawing attention to what appeared to be another set of ornaments.

"It's nothing," she replied, shifting in her rocker as if I had made her uncomfortable.

I noticed the name on the lid. "Who is Charles?" I asked.

"Someone I used to know a long time ago," Lila said matter-of-factly.

"Do I have a brother?" I joked.

"You're not very funny, Sophie," she said crossly. "I told you it was someone I used to know a long time ago. Now, let it settle."

"By the sound of your voice, it's not settled," I replied. I rolled my eyes at her swift change in tone.

Seemingly irritated with my prying, Lila picked up the box and placed it back in the storage chest. From what I knew, she didn't keep anything that didn't mean something to her. In fact, if she kept anything at all, it was most likely an object that triggered a profound memory, one that she wanted to be reminded of often. This was one more mystery that would need further investigation.

Before returning to her rocker, Lila turned on the radio to lighten the mood, and we listened to traditional Christmas music while watching the fire and simply basking in the moment. After a while, Lila began to sing along. I loved her enunciation of words and the unique and soulful way she sang.

"Do you miss her?" I asked soberly.

"Every moment."

"Me too. Do you think she's with us tonight?"

"She's always with us, Sophie. The beauty is I get to see her every day in you."

"That's crazy," I said. "I feel the same way. I mean, I get to see her in you too." Realizing I felt very much at home, I added, "I love this house."

"Home is a place in our heart where love resides," Lila replied. "It isn't a location, and it isn't a structure made of wood or brick. Imagine sitting in front of a warm, cozy fire and feeling a blanket of warmth wrapping you without judgment or shame. Or butterflies fluttering amid a clear blue sky and birds singing a song only you can understand. Home is where your heart rests with God."

I laid my head back down beside Hunner and knew that this would be a Christmas to remember. I was a girl believing again, hope was in sight, and for the first time today, I prayed. I prayed that this moment would never end. As Lila often said, "Life's joys and miracles are in moments." For me, those moments were happening more and more often, or at least now, I was able to recognize and appreciate them.

Though a good time, this was also a time of sadness for Lila and me because we both missed Mom so much. Everything was finally coming together in my life, but the ache in my heart for Mom never stopped. In the beginning, we didn't talk of her much, I suppose, because it was too painful. I thought she was so beautiful. Her hair was long and ash brown, which looked like a mixture of Lila's dark brown hair and the blond in mine. When I looked into Mom's eyes, I could almost see into the depths of her soul. She was smart and funny, and I loved her soft smile, just like Lila's. She was perfect in my eyes.

She wasn't afraid to let people see who she was, whether they liked her or not. She was a free spirit sailing in life's ocean, and I wanted so badly to be sailing with her. I missed her so much that at times, I tried not to think about her. I was afraid if I started crying, I would never stop. She was never coming home.

Lila and I shared this Christmas together, making the greatest attempt to displace the painful memories in our hearts so that we could survive another holiday. We ended Christmas Day with a prayer, and before retiring to our bedrooms, Lila came across the hallway and reached out to me.

I ran into her arms and held on to her with all my might. *Don't let me go,* I thought to myself. *Please, don't ever let me go.*

Lila held on to me with the same passion, and in silence and reflection of the day, we let go quietly and retreated to our rooms.

When I reached my bedroom door, Lila stopped me. "Sophie, it's okay," she said gently. "Across the morning sky, all the birds are singing. They know when it's time for them to go, just as your mother knew it was her time. When you hear the birds sing, you'll know that it's her singing to you. Sweet dreams, dear."

Closing my bedroom door, I quickly jumped from the cold floor to my heavenly bed and lay on my back staring out the window. The night seemed surreal. Ice particles had frozen on portions of the windows, and as the light from the cold moon shone through and splashed upon my face, the thought of Mom was foremost in my mind. The sadness began to leave, and with each thought of Lila and Mom, I began to feel warmer, warmer than I had ever felt in my life.

For so long, I had felt betrayed, and instead of dealing with the pain, I used it against myself and others. I couldn't forgive Mom for leaving me. I loved her so much, and there were still so many things that I wanted to do with her, to tell her, to share. I wanted more shopping trips, more walks in the park, afternoon dances in the rain, cuddling in her arms at night, picking flowers, laughing at her jokes, morning hugs. I wanted more time. I saw her in my dreams, but when I reached for her, she faded away into a beautiful white light while I continued to reach with all my might.

Now my feelings and emotions were slowly breaking through, and the bricks were falling one by one from the wall of pain that I had built around myself. I was sorry for being so angry at her. I was sorry for being angry at God. My one wish was that God would let her hear me say, "I'm sorry." Those two words had been locked up in my heart by anger, and Lila had taken the key and set them free. My stubbornness had cheated me out of my own happiness, and I now understood. I had wanted many times to surrender, but my heart was hard, filled with hate, filled with hurt. Unable to unravel the feelings, I had remained in a prison of my own despair.

I continued to stare out the window, my eyes full of tears, my heart full of love. Drifting peacefully off to sleep, I thought of one more mystery: *Who is Charles?*

The cold remained heavy in the Nebraska countryside, and Lila and I became closer with each passing day. With our short conversations, we took baby steps toward one another. Yet our secrets of the past remained our own, and we allowed each other the privacy and space we needed. The years of separation from one another somehow felt like a torn blanket, one Lila began quietly mending. With each stitch, she seemed to be putting our hearts back together.

I was beginning to see how much alike we really were. She was a tough cookie who didn't take any crap off others, yet she held a grace that I couldn't touch. I was a tough cookie, but the crumbs were all over the floor, and I needed the peace that she held as if she had complete ownership of it. Lila wasn't anything that I had imagined she would be or could have ever believed in if I had.

Chapter 9

Spring was in sight, and Hunner and I were both ready to get back outside where we belonged, where we felt most comfortable. School was bearable, but if it weren't a necessary requirement, I could've found much better things to do with my time. It wasn't easy making friends there, and I could hardly blame that on anyone but myself. I focused on homework and sat alone at lunch with my thoughts, and although they were sometimes as warped as people, they were certainly safer.

I couldn't help but notice when the girls made fun of me, whispering back and forth to one another and pointing fingers with malicious enjoyment. Lila once said that when someone is spewing words of contempt and untruth about others, it's because they themselves have not yet found the truth. Even under the roof of the Lord, envious that she couldn't replicate Lila's fresh-baked bread, Lou Lou Bell quickly turned up her nose—so much so, I believed she would kill for the secret of that bread! More and more, I was witnessing people wanting to outdo each other instead of doing for each other, and I couldn't believe for a moment that this was what God had intended for any of us. I watched people quick to falsely judge others because of their own identity malfunctions. There was still a part of me that wanted to kick ass on the girls at school who snickered and stared.

But as Lila said, "When you roll in the mud with the pigs, you're just another dirty pig." I had to agree with her, and since I was still under custody of the court and living in her home, I had to be on my best behavior. The farm had grown on me, and the last thing I wanted to do was to jeopardize the only place I had come to love since my home in River Crossing.

To my surprise and delight, Blake became my saving grace at school. I looked forward to seeing him, and though he didn't know it, I even went out of my way to pass him in the hallway and waited by my locker hoping he would accompany me to the bus. I was attracted to his kindness as well as to his good looks. His vibrant smile made it nearly impossible not to smile back. His smile was wide but not too wide, just perfect. Quite often, when I saw that smile, I found myself in a stupor for several minutes, trying to wipe the grin off my face. Unfortunately, he had that effect on most of the girls at school.

Every feature of his face appeared to have been beautifully sculpted. I loved his brown eyes and long dark lashes. His ears were small, and his dark brown hair, sometimes tucked behind them, fell perfectly into place. Easy on the eyes would be an understatement—he was dessert for the eyes. Sometimes, I would become so absorbed that I didn't even notice he was looking back at me. My fear was that if he ever found out who I really was, what I was really like, he would never smile at me again. Blake was modest, but he had to know that every girl at school had her heart set on him. I was quietly jealous, knowing that his would never be set on mine.

The cold of winter and lazy days in front of the warmth of the fire were fading away to welcome the arrival of spring. Lila and I shared many of the household chores, and I was beginning to learn more about what needed to be done on the farm. Hunner continued to be my constant companion and followed every step I took, except when I had to go to school. Then, he would sadly sit and watch me climb into the bus with his big brown eyes, leaving me guilt-ridden as we drove out of sight. In the evening, we would retreat to the hay barn, where I would rub behind his ears, lay my head down on his thick brown coat, and look up into the sky to daydream.

Life had become full of surprises, and I was discovering new things about myself, including my love of writing. Lila suggested I keep a journal to express my thoughts and dreams so that one day I could look back and see how far I had come. I began my journal, and every evening as I lay in bed, I finished the day with writing. Words poured from my mind onto the paper. No longer locked away and hidden, every emotion and every dream that I was waiting to have come true were expressed in my journal.

I found myself in new territory when I began writing a second letter to Gabe retracting my feelings. My heart was restless as we still had a lot of unfinished business. I was beginning to miss him less and less with each passing day, and there were days that I forgot about him altogether. With that, I was finding peace with resolution.

His control of me had been consciously bestowed with the use of fear. I realized I wasn't a victim of an innocent mistake. I was a fool to allow real actions to replace false words. I no longer loved him and was certain that I never really had. Fear had consumed my life for the past few years, and I was choosing to be free. I prayed that the letter I sent to Gabe when I first arrived on the farm had been intercepted. But I wasn't satisfied with wishful thinking, and although I hadn't heard from him in several months, there was still a chance that he would come for me. I wasn't merely a fool for telling him where I was—I had wrapped the rope around my neck and tied it for him. Placing the second letter to Gabe along with my journal, I stuffed it between the mattress and box springs for safekeeping until I could get it mailed.

With every passing day and night, the breeze rolled in with warmer air, and the sun stayed a little longer. I thought the essence of the farm was something that every child should know. I only wished that I had known it sooner. But I felt blessed, and I was changing with the seasons. My sadness was being lifted with love from Hunner and Lila and the farm.

Chapter 10

Spring had finally arrived, and the cycle was starting all over again. Flowers were fresh with hypnotic fragrance as they danced toward the sun. Earth's coat was turning into a luscious green carpet, small buds from the bushes and trees were beginning to appear, and all of earth's creatures were waking from a long-needed sleep. It was as if Mother Nature slowly opened the eyes of each of her majestic wonders, and the farm held many.

Farmers in the county were soon busy planting the fields, and the rest was in God's hands. Lila assigned me the chore of planting the farm garden. *This would be interesting at best*, I thought. The only planting I had done until now was my ass in a seat.

Lila presented me with seed packets.

"Seriously," I scoffed. "That's like handing a baby a pack of cigarettes."

"I have complete faith in you, Sophie," she replied encouragingly, sensing my resistance. "All the tools you need are in the shed. Other than those tools and your seeds, all you need is a little love from Mother Nature."

After some brief instructions from Lila, I successfully planted my first garden. Although the rows were a bit crooked, I was proud to have completed the task and hoped that soon the plants would begin showing. I planted squash, onions, tomatoes, beans, cucumbers, and a few other things that were a mystery to me.

I was excited by the thought of watching the garden grow. Robert talked so eloquently about the pride he took in planting his farm; I hoped that even I could achieve this small step. Each day, I meticulously cared for the garden, making sure to water and hoping that the sun would do its part. After a few weeks, Lila and I walked to the garden together so that I could show her the first small sprouts pushing their way through the soil.

She bent over to pluck a few weeds, and then studied the garden as if she were looking at a piece of art. Wiping her forehead with her glove, she carefully lowered herself to the ground and sat down beside the garden. "Every year, it gets harder and harder to get up and down," she said with disgust. Pulling her knees to her chest, she sat peacefully and looked far beyond the farm. "Let me tell you a story, Sophie," she said, patting the ground beside her as a signal for me to take a seat.

Sitting beside her, I listened intently. It seemed as if every word she spoke spilled from her heart so quickly that it left her little room to breathe.

"Your grandfather's favorite place was right here beside this garden," she said with joy in her voice. "He was so proud of his cucumbers, always saying that he raised the best in the county." She laughed. "He would come here every day and carefully manicure the garden, pulling the weeds and making sure bugs weren't eating away at his prize possessions. One day, I watched him as he gathered the vegetables into the basket. He held the tomatoes and cucumbers up to the sun, studying them as if they were alive. And, Sophie, that's the true beauty, something I had never realized before: he could see more than just the vegetables. He saw his contribution to God. He had been given the gift of land and the seeds to create nourishment for our bodies, and that pleased him, in return nourishing his soul. He truly loved every moment on the farm, and I loved that about him. When I watch you here in the garden, it pleases my heart." She smiled.

"Am I missing something?" I asked. "From the first day I set foot on this farm, I've felt nothing but peace, and each day, I feel better than the day before. But I also feel like I've been cheated. How could my mother leave such an incredible place and keep me away from grandparents that loved me so much? I don't understand any of this. I want to know what happened. I *need* to know what happened. Please trust me enough now to tell me."

I couldn't read Lila's expression, and she remained silent. She sighed. "It's a long story, so we better get comfortable," she said, while rearranging herself on the ground.

"Please start from the beginning."

"Do you remember me telling you that I grew up in New York?"

"Yeah, I remember that."

"Well, let's start with how I arrived in Morton Falls," she continued. "Shortly after high school graduation, I received a letter from my father's brother, Walt Rasmussen, and his wife, Katie, who lived in Morton Falls, Nebraska. Katie swore she had been cursed because she and Will, his nickname for short, weren't able to have children. Uncle Will was a tall, thin, good-looking man who had arrived in America a few years prior to my parents' arrival. He quickly began processing documents to secure his future as a United States citizen. The cute, curly-headed blonde who politely offered her assistance as he stood in line soon became Kate Rasmussen. They were an interesting couple. Will whistled constantly, and Katie sang. Unfortunately, neither of them was good at either. Five minutes in their company, and you were nearly driven mad." Lila chuckled. "However annoying, though, you couldn't help but love them. They treated me like I was their own child, and God was incredibly generous, blessing me with more love than I probably deserved.

"It was May of 1956 when a tornado more than a mile wide swept through part of the Midwest, destroying everything in its path. Farms and livestock were swept away as if they hadn't even existed. Will and Katie's farm was directly in the path of the tornado, and they lost everything except their lives. Katie wrote to my mother requesting that I come to Morton Falls for the summer to help rebuild their farm. It certainly wasn't what I had planned after graduation. I envisioned endless days on the beach spent soaking up the sun and evenings amid gorgeous men under the flirtatious moon. I wanted to breathe. I had been dreaming of this summer all year, and I was ready to go wherever the wind took me—but not to Nebraska!"

"I can totally relate to that," I spat out.

"I argued with my parents, just like any other normal young teenager, about what I was going to do after graduation. They wanted me to go to college, but I wanted to live for a little while without restriction. Daddy's meat shop had become a huge success, and we were busier than we could manage. Mother and I worked the shop, but it wasn't something I could see myself doing long-term. I was still trying to figure out who I was, and I hadn't given much thought to what I wanted to become. You could almost say, Sophie, that I was spoiled. Life had been pretty comfortable for me up to this point. I wanted it to last longer.

"I read Katie's letter over and over and finally came to a conclusion: I wouldn't be able to live with myself if I didn't help them. Regardless of what I wanted, I didn't see any other option, so I started packing. At first, I was hesitant, but the truth is, there were other issues presenting themselves, which helped motivate my decision to leave. The neighborhood where I had grown up was once quiet, and neighbors watched out for one another, just like they do here. But it wasn't safe anymore. More and more often, we heard stories of young women being raped and even murdered. The streets were becoming dangerous and no place for a young woman. I was fearless, Mother reminded me, to a fault. I hadn't made the best choices when it came to young men, and my heart had been broken many times. I was a fool for love, and therefore...foolish," Lila said it with regret.

"That makes two of us," I said. We both laughed, and even though it wasn't something to brag about, we found common ground in being human.

"As you would say, Sophie, I was a 'loser magnet,'" she continued, as if she were still trying to convince herself of her decision. "I needed to get out of the city. I needed a change—I needed *to* change. My mother convinced me that it was only for a summer, and it would be a great place for me to clear my head. It's crazy, Sophie, what lies ahead for each of us. I was only supposed to be there for a short summer." She paused. "Well, that summer turned into a lifetime. I boarded the train from New York City, and within only a few miles of the station, I became sick to my stomach with the thought of the unknown. The long train ride felt like an eternity, and I could already hear Will whistling and Katie singing.

"But as we approached the Midwestern states, my anxiety was replaced with excitement. I looked out the window, and for miles and miles, there were open fields extending as far as the eye could see. I hadn't encountered this much land in all my life. The dull gray concrete was gone, and there was nothing to obstruct the eye from seeing to the horizon of this incredible land.

"As the train pulled into the station, Will and Katie were eagerly awaiting me. As soon as we stopped, I jumped from the train and took in a long, deep breath. I was overcome with my first smell of fresh country air. You will never smell air like that in the city. The three of us piled into the cab of Will's pickup, which had been severely beaten and bruised by the flying debris of the tornado, and headed to their farm. I sat by the window and rolled it down, sticking my head out and taking in all the scents of the clean Nebraska air. I felt like a child smelling a flower for the first time. Aunt Katie found me entertaining as we drove. 'Be careful not to get a bug in your mouth,' she told me.

"My eyes were filled with delight as colors of the land and sky ran into one another. Everything was new and fascinating to me. I realized how shallow I had been in thinking that the only place God inhabited was the one where I had lived. Within a few minutes of jumping from the train, I had fallen in love with something other than the wrong man: I fell in love with the country. The tallest skyscraper in New York couldn't compare to the beauty of a large oak tree.

"Will and Katie's farmstead was situated right over there, about a quarter of a mile." Lila raised her arm and pointed north from where we were sitting. "Today, you can only see a few physical reminders of where it was located. But I can see it clearly in my mind as if it were still there. Fallen bricks and old weathered pieces of boards scattered across the old farmstead now leave traces of the past. Tornadoes destroyed their farm twice. I spent my entire summer helping to rebuild their house and surrounding buildings after the first tornado. Neighbors and town folk were generous in donating their time, and with good old-fashioned hard work and Christian efforts, the farm was back in operation by fall. Several years later, the farm was hit again by a second tornado, and Will and Katie just didn't have the passion or the will to start all over again. They had worked hard all their lives and were simply tired.

"Katie had always said one day she would go back home to the East Coast. She wanted to be closer to her family, and Will's arthritis was becoming more and more severe with the cold Nebraska weather. In their desperation, they looked about their twisted and torn farm, and realizing it was more than they could handle, they left. It was a sad day for many people in Morton Falls when they departed.

"I promise this is all leading somewhere," Lila said with an endearing smile. She began speaking proudly about Joseph. "Your grandfather, named after his father, Joseph Lee Randolph II, was a second-generation farmer working this land. I met him the summer I came to help rebuild Uncle Walt's farm. You're familiar with the pond between the Taylors and Gerards?"

I nodded in acknowledgment. Words escaped me as I listened closely to Lila's story, absorbing every word.

"That's where I met Joe. I noticed him one afternoon as he was fishing along the bank of the pond. I had been watching from afar for quite a long time, hoping he wouldn't notice me. When I realized that he'd seen me, I jumped to my feet and ran. He was far faster than I, and he caught me." Lila chuckled. "He grabbed me from behind, and we both fell forward and slid through the tall grass. I squirmed and demanded that he let me go. Of course, when I saw how handsome he was, I surely didn't mean it. We both brushed ourselves off and then stood staring awkwardly at one another. He was so playful." Lila sighed, recalling her memories of him. "'Whatcha lookin' at?' he asked me sarcastically.

"'Nothing!' I sharply replied back.

"He dusted his hat off on his pant leg and then just up and left, walking away laughing to himself."

"He just left you?" I asked, surprised.

"He just left," Lila replied matter-of-factly. "I stood there dumbfounded as he walked out of my sight. A few days later, I ran into him again as work was beginning on Will and Katie's farm. The Randolph family was generous in their services, and they helped out just like most of the other good folk in the county. Joseph proved to be a hard worker and very, let me repeat, very handsome." She smiled. "He had the bluest eyes I had ever seen and curly brown hair to match the farmer's tan that enhanced all the crevices of his sculpted body. One evening after we had all worked hard on the farm, he invited me to go fishing with him. He set the bait, and I was hooked." She laughed at her little joke. "The pond became our special place, and on hot summer nights, we would strip down and swim."

"Ms. Lila! Did I hear that right?" I teased.

"Joseph was raised to be a polite and kind young man, but that didn't stop him from getting naked for a swim." She giggled. "He had a gentle spirit that matched his smile. Joseph and I were both only children, so we understood each other's desire and respect for individual freedom. I hadn't met anyone like him, Sophie. When he proposed a few days before my return to New York, I didn't hesitate to accept, though I was fully aware that my life would be spent on this very farm. Joseph would honor his father's wishes to farm the land and pass it on to the next generation—our children.

"It had been a long, hot summer working on the farm, and I couldn't wait to get home to see my folks. Will and Katie knew the Randolph family very well, and they respected one another. It was without question that they were in favor of Joseph's proposal, but what he needed most was my father's permission. We were both nervous, and Joe bit his nails on the entire drive to New York. My mother cried, and my father's eyes welled up with tears as he shook hands with Joseph and gave his blessing. I packed all my belongings in the car, and together, we began our journey to Morton Falls. In a small church in Saint Paul, we were married upon the eve of my twentieth birthday. Sophie, I loved him with all of my heart."

We both stared at the garden, and it felt as if the spirit of Joseph, my grandfather, was with us.

The sound of a tractor coming up the drive drew our attention from the garden and Lila's story.

"It's Robert," Lila said.

"Is that Hilly in the cab?" I noticed her hands waving back and forth.

"Well, how in the world?" Lila said under her breath.

"Do you mean how in the hell did she fit in the cab?" I asked in disbelief.

"Sophie, please watch your language." She sighed as we watched them approach the house. "Yeah, I think that's what I meant."

The tractor came to a stop, and the cab door flew open. Hilly spilled out, with Robert behind her. "I would have brought a cake, but there wasn't enough room in the cab," Hilly shouted cheerfully as they approached us.

"I'm sure it wouldn't have fit," I whispered to Lila.

"Sophie, be nice," she said under her breath.

Robert approached with his ever-so-friendly smile and greeted me with a hug. "Looks like a pretty good garden," he said pleasantly, perusing my work.

"It's Sophie's first garden," Lila replied. "She's worked very hard on it, and I'm very proud of her."

"Don't get too excited," I warned.

"I'm sure you will have a magnificent garden." Robert patted me reassuringly on the shoulder.

"What brings you our way?" Lila asked.

"Robert wanted to show off his new tractor," Hilly boasted. "And we hoped there was some cold lemonade in the fridge."

"There's always cold lemonade in the fridge," Lila replied, turning to head back to the house.

As we approached the house, Hilly went in to get the lemonade while Robert gave Lila and me a brief view of his new tractor. "She thinks with this new large-size cab, she can spend more time with me in the fields," he said, regretfully questioning his purchase.

"You need to buy her a bigger oven, and then tell her you're gonna bake with her," I teased.

"You just saved my life, Sophie." Robert laughed. "You're one smart cookie."

We settled on the porch and Hilly brought out the lemonade and poured a cold glass for everyone. Later on, with evening falling upon us, Robert and Hilly stuffed themselves back into the cab. Hunner followed them down the road as they left. I was sad that Lila's story had been interrupted, but she assured me that we would find another time to continue.

We walked back to the garden to pick up the shovel and other items we had left behind. Suddenly, she turned toward me, and with sadness in her voice, she spoke softly. "Sophie, I know in your heart, you're crying." She paused. "Let the garden help you heal as it healed me. This is your garden." Hat and gloves in her hand, she walked away, looking up to the sky.

I wondered what she was looking for. Sometimes, I wondered about her sanity.

Then I heard her say quietly under her breath, "Dear Lord, have mercy on these vegetables."

The farm had given me back my life. No, the farm had given me life. From that day on, Lila and I treated the garden as if it were a sanctuary for ourselves and the memory of Grandpa. Lila shared stories of their time together on the farm, and I watched her as she talked of him. She was compelling, and I hung on every word she spoke. At times, I would get lost in how beautiful she was. Her hair shimmered in the warmth of the daylight sun, and her spirit was like a fragrance that hypnotizes. I had fallen under her spell.

Chapter 11

Lila and I worked fervently from spring into the early days of summer. Although school was nearing an end for most of the students, I still needed to fulfill the requirements of summer school in order to graduate. There were many things to look forward to as school was coming to a close, and yet there were many things uncertain. I began questioning what was going to happen to me after I graduated and my sentence on the farm was complete. Could I go back to River Crossing?

The thought alone brought an overwhelming sense of fear that I hadn't had since I arrived on the farm. So much had changed in such a short time, repairing all that had gone completely and horribly wrong in a time I wished could be forgotten. Lila promised that God is gracious, and if he could forgive my past, I certainly should be able to. I had finally realized where her peace came from. She didn't dwell on the past, as yesterday was over last night. Nor did she worry about what might never come. She chose to live solely in the moment, as she said, "Just as God intended." I believed now more than ever that she had a direct line to him.

Excitement was in the air at school with the upcoming prom. I was fascinated by the girls' talk I overheard: Who was going with whom? Who was wearing what? And the big question, who was Blake going to ask? I found myself hoping it would be me, all the while knowing that was merely wishful thinking.

If nothing else, the amusement of watching the girls at school make complete asses of themselves as they fought each other in an attempt to win his affection was well worth my time. I wanted to go as badly as anyone else, but I couldn't see myself with anyone other than Blake. I knew I had set my standards higher than I was worthy, but I didn't want to go if I couldn't participate in the fairy tale I had created in my mind. Blake was the prince, and of course, I was Cinderella. Lila was right when she said my imagination was bigger than life itself, but all daydreaming aside, I knew better than anyone that fairy tales don't come true, at least not for me.

Whatever the case, if I wasn't going to prom, I would make sure that Hunner and I had an amazing evening at the lake. Hunner would playfully splash in the cool water, and I would fish until the sun fell. Grandpa's fishing tackle and poles were still in the old shed, and I had been waiting to put them to good use at the pond. I grew up next to the Missouri River, and almost everyone from River Crossing knew how to fish, or at least they always claimed to. Blake was unaware of my love of fishing, but I couldn't think of anything that I'd rather do with him than sit by the pond, soak up the sun, and fish. And of course, I would catch the biggest fish.

My memories of fishing at the river with Mom were special, and I held them very close to my heart. Every Easter, we would take a picnic to the river and spend hours along the banks fishing. We spent those days in the company of each other and God...just as he intended.

Church was the same as usual—absolutely boring. However, I was getting used to the torture. It had become routine—every Sunday, the same old folk, sitting in the same old place, as if they had been granted ownership of that particular seat in the pew. And every Sunday, the same old church ladies walked by with their smug, ugly faces, noses riding high in the air. However, on this particular Sunday, church was anything but boring.

Lila and I took our usual seats. Like everyone else, we had become creatures of habit, sitting in the same place every week. I had often wondered what Lila had ever done to promote such rude behavior from the old bats at church. I had never heard her speak a bad word to or about anyone; to the contrary, she always tried to find the good in people, even when they didn't deserve it. A few times, the old Sophie was ready to fire back at the old bats, but Lila quickly spied the spit in my eyes and gently placed her hand firmly on my leg, conveying the peace of God.

I unwillingly sank back down into the pew. *Such hypocrites,* I thought.

With the tips of their noses placed upright in the air, it's a wonder they didn't trip going down the aisle. Taking their places right up front, they acted as if they were seated in God's lap. They really didn't have a clue. They were in his lap, all right: he had them turned over with their bare asses sticking up as he was giving them a good old-fashioned spanking. I laughed quietly to myself during the service as I kept visualizing this in my mind. I especially laughed at my vision of Lou Lou Bell because she had a pretty large ass. I would have risked going to hell at this point rather than forfeit these visions. They were hilarious, and I decided that if God had any sense of humor, he'd be laughing with me.

The sermon was tolerable, but what I looked forward to most was leaving. We sang the closing hymn and exited the church when out of the corner of my eye, I witnessed Vivian Gerard laughing loudly, almost as if she were trying to be noticed. Standing among a group of women that included Lou Lou Bell Roberts and Beatrice Meyer, Vivian began speaking of Lila, whispering back and forth and staring.

"Why do you even come here?" I questioned Lila curiously.

"I come to worship," she fired back, walking quickly to the truck.

I found myself almost running to keep up with her. She was becoming noticeably agitated as the laughter from the women continued behind us.

"That's enough!" I saw a fire in Lila's eyes that I had never seen before. Turning to confront the women, Lila barreled toward Vivian with the power of a raging bull. Nose to nose, Lila stood confident, and her words shot through Vivian like an arrow piercing through a tree. "You have something to say?" she asked severely.

Vivian's shoulders slumped, and she leaned back as Lila got close enough to lay on a sloppy kiss. Quieted by Lila's rage, the women disbanded, and Vivian almost stumbled backward in an attempt to escape.

Lila proceeded to the pickup, where I stood in awe. My jawbone was hanging open in disbelief.

"Get in the truck now, Sophie," Lila said firmly.

I jumped in the truck, so tickled I almost couldn't breathe.

Lila started the truck and headed out of the parking lot.

"That was so cool," I said excitedly. "You had her Lila, you had her!" I bounced up and down, the adrenaline rushing through every part of my body. "What the hell was that all about? That woman hates you."

"She hates herself," Lila scoffed angrily.

"Lila, we've been coming to church every Sunday, and every Sunday, it's the same thing. I say we quit going to church." I hoped she would buy it.

"Not a chance, Sophie."

"Well then, I think it's only fair that you 'fess up," I commented bravely.

"Sophie, can we leave it alone today?" Lila asked somberly.

Noticing the sadness in her voice and the expression on her face, I retreated to looking out the window. I couldn't keep up with the mysteries at Morton Falls. But I was aware of my impatience and knew that I would need to find answers soon.

With time passing on the farm, my relationship with Lila and God grew closer. Lila was an inspiration to me and others, sharing God's word as if she were his own personal messenger. I wasn't even close to being as refined as she. In fact, I was still pretty rough around the edges. Lila and I continued to go to church, and the old bats continued their incivility, but after Lila's recent confrontation, they were less obvious. I cursed them while Lila prayed for them.

"Sophie, you must have faith," she stated.

"And what exactly would that do for me?" I asked sarcastically.

"Well, you see, these ladies who sit in judgment of me, we have to have faith that they will someday understand that God has faith in them, that he loves them without judgment."

"Well," I said to Lila jokingly, "that would take a real act of God."

I was beginning to put my faith in God. It's almost impossible to live on a farm with its ties to nature and not feel closely connected to him. Everything depended on him: the rain to feed the plants, the sun to lift them from the ground, the trees to shade you when you needed rest and a cool drink of lemonade. The farm was a living testament to his creation.

"I have faith that one day, he will kick the church ladies' asses," I said, grinning.

Lila clearly dismissed my amusement. "There have been many times when my faith has been tested on the farm," she stated seriously. "Life isn't always easy, Sophie, and there are times when we are all challenged in our faith. But that's when God promises that he's standing right beside us. He wants to know that even in the worst of times, when our faith is being tested the most, that we will stand strong looking to him with love in our hearts and the faith to know he will never leave us."

"Thank you for the sermon. I still have faith that he'll kick their asses!" I laughed.

Memories of Mom were ever present on the farm, and Lila and I both needed to have faith that someday those memories would put a smile on our faces and a joy in our hearts, replacing the tears and sadness that had consumed us. Every so often when I passed Lila's room, I saw her sitting in her chair perusing through old photo albums, running her fingers gently over the photos. I couldn't imagine what that was like for her. My heart now hurt more and more for her and less and less for myself. We were both on a journey of healing. We had stopped looking for help; we had stopped looking for answers. Rather, we had faith that, for whatever reason, God had brought us together. We found comfort in that.

Chapter 12

It was a beautiful Sunday afternoon, and after church, Lila and I agreed it would be a perfect day to take Old Blue for a country drive. We swung by the farm to pick up Hunner, as he loved these country rides as much as we did. He would pace back and forth with his head sticking out the side of the truck and his ears flapping with the wind in his face. He was the happiest dog in the world. It was a miracle that he managed to stay in the truck, as well as managing to stay on all fours as Lila proceeded down the unforgiving bumpy country roads.

Lila and I rolled the windows down and recorded this precious day in our minds. We took in the wind that rushed through the cab of the truck. There was a smell of freshness in the air as we rode through God's country, and our thoughts were lost in the past just like the dust we left behind. *Everyone should experience a Sunday like this,* I thought.

Lila pulled Old Blue into a cornfield near the farm. "Let's put the tailgate down," she said, getting out of the truck.

I jumped swiftly onto the tailgate and watched Lila as she struggled to raise herself.

"Damn, I need a new body," she grunted, laughing a little with embarrassment.

We sat quietly, letting the breeze roll across our faces, and listened to the sounds of life.

"The last time we talked by the garden," Lila said, "our conversation was interrupted by the Taylors. I think it's important for you to know what happened...why your mother left. Are you up for a story?"

"Are you kidding?" I replied. "That's like asking me if I need air to breathe." I couldn't wait to hear the rest of her tale.

"Well then, let's get comfortable."

Lila directed me to pull the blanket from behind the truck seat. Placing it in the floor of the bed, we leaned against the cab and looked out into the distance.

"Where did I leave off?" Lila chuckled at her lack of memory.

"I think you and Joseph had just gotten married."

"Oh, that's right," Lila said, clearing her throat before continuing. "The first couple years of our marriage were hard times working the farm, but we loved each other, and we rarely took time to notice. In the evenings, we would sit up in the barn hanging our legs over the side and dream, just like you do, Sophie." She smiled. "Joe always had to put a piece of straw in his mouth and chew on it as he looked out into the distance. He would take my hand in his and, every so often, lean over and kiss me on the cheek.

"Occasionally, we would talk about New York, and I got a sense that Joe worried that someday I would miss it enough to return. There were certainly things that I missed, but I found a peace on the farm that I had longed for. I couldn't get over the smell of the fresh air. Sometimes, I would stand in the middle of the bean field consumed by the ocean of green. Stretching my arms out as if I could fly and looking up into the cloudless sky, I would inhale. I know I must've looked like a fool, but who other than God was watching? In the city, people can buy the best of everything with their money, but standing in that bean field, I had the best God had to offer, and it was free. I was never going to give it up."

We both stayed silent for a moment and gazed out at the landscape.

Lila continued, "In the winter of 1958, as beautiful shimmering snowflakes were twirling in the cold Nebraska wind, we were blessed with your mother. She was everything Joseph and I had dreamed of. She was beautiful. Being pregnant had been extremely difficult for me, but through the grace of God, our baby girl entered the world with everything intact: ten little fingers and ten little toes...perfect! Appropriately, we named her Grace. Everything seemed too good to be true, and it was. We were at the top of the world when we looked into her eyes. Unfortunately, the intensity of our joy was quickly diminished when doctors informed us that I wouldn't be able to have any more children because of complications during my pregnancy. Joe had always wanted a big family, especially boys to pass the farm on to, but it didn't change how much he loved Gracie.

"She looked so much like you when you were born, with her ocean-blue eyes, soft golden blond hair that felt like silk, and rosy pink cheeks. She was definitely Daddy's little girl and had him wrapped around her finger. From the moment he laid eyes on her, he was hooked. I'm sure there were times when Joe was sad that we couldn't have more children. Heck, there were times when I was sad. However, our lives were full, and I was thankful that God had given us Grace.

"From the time I was a little girl, my mother had taught me how to appreciate the wonderful things God had given us, rather than to look at what he had not. She used to say, 'Lila, don't wear yourself out trying to fill your basket. He promises it will always be full.' I needed a lot of her wisdom and faith on the farm.

"Daily tasks filled up every moment of the day. The farm always needed tending to: trading eggs and grocery shopping in town, sewing, and of course, church on Sunday. We had settled into a peaceful life, though routine and predictable, and at times, even boring. Each year brought new challenges on the farm, and we quickly learned that we had no control of life itself. All we could hope for was that everything we survived would come with a strength we once thought impossible to find."

Leaning up against the cab, I focused my eyes intently on Lila. With each word, her story grew, and I was beginning to see, to understand, the depth of her love and her strength. I had come to love her more than I ever thought possible. Once in a dream, I stood watching the ocean, and I became hypnotized as God blew the waves upon the beach and, without notice, stole my soul as the water gently pulled me back into the ocean. Lila's love was that of the ocean. She continued telling her story as if she were reciting a novel.

"Gracie was growing up so fast on the farm. I can still see her trailing behind Joe as he fed the livestock or chasing after the tractor as he headed for the fields." Lila smiled broadly. "Wise beyond her age, she wasn't a pushover. She gave new meaning to *independence*." She chuckled. "Although she loved the farm as a little girl, the older she got, Joe and I could see that her interests were elsewhere. Her dream was to open an art studio in a large city and display her paintings. I'm not sure where she inherited her artistic talent. The only thing Joe and I knew how to paint was a barn. Nonetheless, she had a God-given gift, and all we wanted was to help her succeed. She and I used to joke that we were both born in the wrong place. She preferred the energy and excitement of a big city, and I preferred the simplicity of the country.

"There is much to love on a farm," Lila continued softly, "but there are many sacrifices. I missed my parents and my aunt and uncle so much. Joe promised I could return home each year, but it was nearly impossible with so many duties waiting." A long sigh escaped Lila's lips. "The farm was exhausting at times. I woke early in the morning before the sun even had a chance to rise, and I woke the rooster. Then I fell into bed long after the sun retired. The best part of the day was lying on the old feather bed mattress as my worn and tired body calmed itself in its comfort.

"Our days of dreaming in the barn were replaced with conversations that included how much feed to buy, who was taking the eggs to town, and planting schedules. Just as if you overwater a plant, it will die, I found myself saturated with details and felt like I was dying. Joe and I started to resemble business partners, rather than husband and wife. We became physical bodies moving in the present, but wishing and hoping to reclaim some of the magic that we had felt for each other in the past.

"At night, I lay in bed, staring out the window, gazing at the moon. I questioned who I had become and fantasized about who I wanted to be. The fantasy, unfortunately, had to be put in a box and placed on a shelf in my mind as I was fully aware that I had accepted the life I had chosen. We live with the choices we make every day, Sophie, so consider those choices carefully. There will be times when things won't turn out the way you had wished or planned them to be, but you then realize you made the best decision you could at the time."

I could see the sadness in her face and wished I could do something to wipe it away.

"I had accepted the life I chose," Lila said, "but I didn't know if I could accept the loneliness. I began to feel as if I were a ghost, unseen but still present. Perception is replaced by truth, especially in a small town. From the outside looking in, it appeared that Joe and I had everything. And that's the real question: What is everything? Is it a house, a car, money, beautiful children running about?

"By looking at us, you couldn't see the truth. We went to church together every Sunday, and as I sat there looking around the room, I wondered what other people's lives were like. I wondered if they were going through the same loneliness I was. My mind quite often drifted from the sermon into fantasy, and oh, my Lord, if he knew what was running through my mind, I certainly would have been expelled from church!" Lila laughed.

I laughed too. Maybe I wasn't the only one who sometimes felt I didn't belong in church.

Lila lowered her eyes. "I was once a vibrant young woman, a lot like you, Sophie, ready to take on the world. Don't get me wrong. Your grandpa was a good man. He was a loving father to Grace and a good provider. Our desires just became separate from our actions. I needed and wanted more from him. I wanted to feel like a woman. I think after so many years, I looked more like a farmhand than his wife, and I desperately wanted him to chase me around the farm, laughing like he used to. I wanted to sit in the barn dreaming of places we would go, talking of romantic trips to faraway places. I wanted him to hold my hand more, kiss me more, touch me more...love me more."

I leaned over and gently kissed Lila on the forehead, acknowledging my compassion for her. Lila accepted my kiss with a gentle smile. I was quiet as a mouse as her story continued. I was enthralled by every word and didn't want to miss a thing.

"Things didn't get much better," she said sadly. "Joe took over full control of the family farm as a result of his father's passing, and the pressure began to escalate even more than it had before until Joe no longer resembled any part of the man I once knew. Responsibilities were endless with a big farm, and as you well know, there was always work to be done. There wasn't time to worry about how we felt. Our bodies were tired, our hands calloused and worn. We both lost sight of the one thing that should have been the most important—one another.

"Joe and I began sleeping in separate beds to rest more comfortably, which eventually led to a complete lack of intimacy between the two of us. After a while, it became a normal way of life. Lying in my old iron bed alone, I watched as the light from the moon drifted off into the heavens, and I prayed. I asked God to give me the strength to make it through another day. I fell asleep knowing that tomorrow was always a new day of hope, and that sustained me."

When I watched Lila's eyes well up with tears, my heart grew sad. I had no words.

Lila took a deep breath. "Are you okay?" she asked.

I was always amazed by her thoughtfulness of others. "I'm fine," I said, choking back tears. I wanted her story to go on.

"Before I knew it, Grace was a beautiful seventeen-year-old young woman, turning the heads of every young man she passed. She had the spirit of a wild filly and lived each day as if the wind were her guide. Her laugh was contagious, and when I think of her, that is definitely what I miss the most. Life on a farm is not for everyone, and it wasn't the life for Grace. Chores were brutal, or at least that's what she thought. If she had used even a little of the energy she used complaining, she would have had her work done in half the time. Joe was becoming less and less tolerant of her flippant attitude and unrealistic ideals, and their relationship began to slowly go downhill. Eventually, they barely spoke to one another.

"Still, we loved Grace so much, and we tried everything we could to reason with her. She spent most of her time with her friends in Saint Paul, and we rarely saw her on the farm. It would be an understatement to say she had a strong will. I found myself in uncomfortable territory refereeing between her and Joe, and usually by the time it was all over, they were both angrier with me than they had been with each other. I couldn't win."

Lila looked so defeated, I wished I could think of a way to comfort her.

"I once held this sweet little baby girl in my arms and closed my eyes as I rocked her, envisioning every wonderful part of her life. Not for one moment did I ever think that I could make her so angry that she wouldn't want me to be a part of it. Grace confessed to me that she would never live in the prison I had confined myself to and that she had lost all respect for me. I had lost her because of who I had become. It angers me that she was right."

As Lila spoke of my mother and her life on the farm, it felt like she had opened a book I had been waiting to read for years, and I wanted nothing more than for her to continue on.

"Nothing could prepare us for what was going to happen next," Lila said, an expression of pain on her face. "Grace graduated from high school and began looking at colleges to attend in the fall. Some were nearby, and some were halfway across the United States—the ones she favored most. I think she had finally convinced me that getting as far away from Morton Falls as possible would be the best thing for her, even though in my heart, I wanted to keep her as close as I could. I knew it would be hard to see Grace leave, but I wanted nothing more than to see her succeed. I believed in her. I knew she could accomplish whatever she set out to do.

"So you can only imagine how shocked we were when she came home one hot summer evening to tell us she was pregnant. Devastated for her, I stood frozen, unable to react. What was I to say to her? What did she expect me to say? It was certainly too late to do anything. I just stood there for a moment, speechless.

"Joe's reaction was quite different. Anger got the best of him, which was certainly out of character. I had never seen him that out of control. He began shouting at her. She shouted back. Neither of them made any sense at all, and words that should never have been spoken were thrown at each other like arrows through the heart." Lila paused for a moment and lowered her head.

"Take your time," I said. I wasn't sure she would be able to go on.

After a few minutes of silence, she asked carefully, "Sophie, do you know who your father is?"

"A little bit," I replied, hoping to let her know I wanted her to continue.

"Well, his name is John Christiansen. I have to admit, he was quite handsome, with dirty blond hair and deep blue eyes. You wouldn't find a girl in Saint Paul who hadn't tried to win over his affection. Your mother and John had known each other most of their lives. They started out despising each other, which I think ultimately led to their attraction. They began dating when they were juniors in high school and became nearly inseparable, attached at the hip, for the next few years.

"It was no secret that Joe wasn't fond of John, but we hoped that the relationship would run its course and Gracie would go her own way after she graduated. John was from a wealthy family in Saint Paul who used their money to buy influence, not to mention to purchase other things that money wasn't meant to buy, if you know what I mean. He had nothing to offer Grace and hadn't worked a hard day in his life. Everything was handed to him. Your grandfather believed that hard work built character in a man, and that if you took something for nothing, you became exactly that—nothing. I couldn't stay silent anymore as the two of them took shots at one another. Once again the referee, I knew I was putting myself in the line of fire, but I jumped in, knowing I would ultimately be the one to get burned.

"Joe shouted for me to get out of the way. After I refused several times, he simply pushed me aside, grabbed Gracie by her neck, and pinned her head up against the wall. He promised to cut off all ties with her and her unborn child and told her she wasn't welcome in his home. The words still tear at my heart. The look of fear and shame in her eyes still haunts my memory. It took everything I had to get him to release his hands from her neck. I then found myself standing alone as Grace ran to her room crying and Joe retreated to the barn. Neither of them noticed I was dying inside.

"Grace and Joe both went to bed that evening without a word to me or to one another. Though not altogether unusual, this time there was little doubt that they would still not be talking in the morning. Our family was at a crossroads, and I didn't have the answers for either of them, the strength to pray for them, or the energy to console them.

"The next morning, Grace rose early. She wasted no time packing up belongings from her room and running through the house, hastily grabbing items to take with her. She seemed to have no idea where she was going or what she was going to do, but she nevertheless insisted that she would be leaving the farm for good. I desperately wanted her and Joe to make amends before she left and begged her to stay until he arrived after completing his chores. I hoped that if she would stay a few more minutes to talk to him, it would change things, but nothing I said altered her relentless will to leave.

"I heard John's truck come roaring up the driveway and the sound of Grace dragging her luggage and large trash bags of personal belongings down the steps. Through the house, she quickly made her way out the back kitchen door where John was waiting. I yelled for her to wait for her father and chased her every last step to John's truck.

"You know, Sophie, I have replayed that scene in my mind a million times, and it took a million times to realize I couldn't have changed a thing. Life changes in a moment. These moments define us in many ways: they can be lessons, they can make us better, they can bring us great happiness or great sorrow, or they can define whether we live or die.

"Earlier that morning, Joe came to the kitchen. He was heartbroken. He looked worn and tired as a result of staying up all night reliving over and over in his mind things he had said and done the prior evening. He was eager to find the right words to repair what had been broken. A humbled man, he confessed to me how much he loved Grace and that he would do everything he could to help her. His anger the night before had been a result of the fear he felt for her. He was scared for her and also for her unborn child. Knowing how harsh this world can be, he knew it wouldn't be easy for her." Lila spoke sadly, recalling the memories of the past. "The last thing he said to me that morning was how sorry he was that he had hurt Grace. He humbly apologized to me before slamming the kitchen door behind him as he left to do his chores.

"Outside, John was incredibly annoying as he laid on the horn. I continued to plead with Grace to talk to her father before she left. Refusing to listen, she threw her remaining bag into John's truck, and they sped recklessly down the driveway as if fleeing a fire.

"The only thing on Joe's mind that morning was making things right with Gracie, so naturally when he, still on his tractor, saw John's truck racing down the drive, he quickly turned the tractor, forgetting he was pulling a trailer behind him loaded with hay. The abrupt turn of the tractor and the weight of the trailer caused the tractor to capsize." Lila choked as tears began flowing down her cheeks. "Joe was under the tractor, and he was killed instantly. I can see it in my mind as clearly as if it happened only moments ago. He was taken away from me that quickly.

"I thought about how ungrateful I had been, how we had spent the last several years ignoring each other's feelings. How could he have known what I was feeling if I never told him? Now I would never get the chance to tell him. He was gone. Sometimes, we don't get second chances." Lila wiped the tears from her cheeks. Taking my hand in hers, she squeezed it tightly. "Promise me you will be quick to forgive and grateful for what God has given you."

"I will," I replied. "I promise."

We rearranged ourselves in the truck bed, trying to get more comfortable, and Lila continued on. "The church was full as hundreds of friends and family attended Joe's funeral. The outpouring of love was overwhelming, and many wondered how a man who had worked so many years on a farm without an injury could be so careless he would capsize his tractor. They didn't realize that Joe had his sights set on Gracie. He couldn't imagine her leaving without telling her he was sorry and how much he loved her. Nothing else existed in that moment—nothing.

"It didn't take long for people to figure out that Gracie was pregnant, despite her best attempts to conceal her growing belly. With Joe gone, she stayed with me at the farm for the next several months and rarely went into town, hoping to escape the disparaging remarks and disapproving stares from our lovely friends, the church ladies. Because they never saw her, people thought she had already left.

"Joe's absence on the farm left a huge void to fill. Nothing could have prepared me for the work that needed to be done, and no one would have been able to understand my despair. Grace did everything she could to help me, but soon, she was too big and too exhausted to help with even the menial tasks.

"I missed Joe every day, but I found joy as I watched your mother grow bigger and bigger every day in anticipation of a new life. I felt like I had something to look forward to, and my hope was restored. Your grandfather was a smart man, and he hit the nail on the head regarding John. Joe knew he was barely capable of taking care of himself, let alone anyone else, and now with the prospect of a wife and child, John became less and less available. While Grace anxiously awaited your arrival, he awaited the next round of golf. It didn't take him long to leave her once he figured out staying with her would cramp his style. She was devastated. On top of the guilt she felt, believing that her father's death was her fault, the only way she thought she could survive was to leave the farm.

"The day you arrived, December 22, 1980, was bitter cold. The prior evening's winter storm had created a blinding display of ice particles covering every part of the farm. Roads were ice-covered, but Old Blue, which we really should name Old Reliable, got us to the hospital in the nick of time. Outside of my own daughter's birth, it was one of the greatest days of my life. I was in the delivery room with your mother, and nothing can describe the joy and awesome wonder I experienced seeing you take your first breath. The doctor had your little feet pinned between his fingers, and holding you almost upside down in the air, he gave a tap to your bottom. Sounding much like a baby pig, you let out a grunt—not a cry, a grunt." Lila laughed. "A real farm girl had been born."

I wasn't amused that I was being compared to a farm animal, especially a pig. *Why couldn't I have sounded more like a horse?* I thought.

"I said you sounded like a pig, not that you looked like one." Lila chuckled.

"Well, that's a relief," I replied, laughing a bit. I knew Lila was only joking.

"The doctor handed you to me while they took care of your mother. I looked into your eyes and you into mine, and we were bonded for life. It was a special bond that I couldn't explain. Even though impossible, it was as if I had known you all of my life. When your mother looked into your eyes, you gave new meaning to her: you gave her life.

"After you were born, I desperately pleaded with Grace to stay with me on the farm. I knew all too well that once she left, there was the great possibility that she would not return. Her guilt and shame were far stronger than I had anticipated. When she left, she was gone forever, and so were you. I rarely heard from her, and she refused to give me an address, knowing that I would definitely try to find her and persuade her to come home.

"I don't believe she ever got over feeling responsible for Joe's death, and she couldn't look at me, knowing that she had taken him from me. Years of words unspoken were a crime against both of us. I know she made mistakes. We all do. But time isn't something we can get back or replace, that's why it's so precious. Sometimes, I still find myself being angry with Grace," Lila said sadly, a hint of bitterness on her tongue. "I missed your birthday parties. I missed everything.

"My loneliness on the farm rose to a level far beyond what I thought I could survive. I became numb moving upon the land,

and there were times when I questioned whether I could make it through another day. I cursed God and asked him to take the very breath he had given me. Days seemed to run into one another, and before I knew it, many years had passed. I had been where you were when we finally met. I, too, once questioned my faith and belief in God. I couldn't reconcile these feelings, so I prayed, and eventually, I found my way back to God, my way back to peace, and I found love again.

"About the time I thought I had it all together, I received a call from one of your mother's coworkers at the hospital, informing me that your mother had died. She told her coworker that she was to call me only in the event of her death, but by no means did she want me to know beforehand that she had cancer. If it weren't for knowing that you were out there somewhere, I believe I would have taken my own life that day."

Lila and I both sat silently. I was numb. Although the mystery had been unraveled as to why my mother had left the farm, I was angry at her for not having the courage to fix what she had broken. She had not only removed herself from the love of her mother, she had robbed me of my grandmother.

Lila looked up into the sky and thanked God for her life. She looked at me closely. "Are you okay?"

"Not really, but I want to hear the rest."

"All right," she said. "I arrived in River Crossing a few days before Grace's funeral. I asked the funeral director and anyone I came in contact with where I could find you, but no one knew where you were staying. I was sure I would find you at the funeral, but the funeral director told me you left abruptly after the service. I stayed in River Crossing for a few more weeks searching for you relentlessly, but to no avail. You weren't at school, you weren't registered with the local city or state officials. It was as if you had vanished.

"Then one evening, the farm was as still as I had ever seen it. The clouds were moving gently through the blue sky with a wind carrying all the scents of the land. I took a deep breath and prayed that somehow we would be reunited. I sat back in my old wicker chair on the porch and began dreaming of what it would be like to see you again. I asked God for a miracle. In the middle of my prayer, the phone rang. It was the judge from River Crossing. He told me everything that you had gone through and what had happened after you were left in foster care. I wish I would have known." Lila wiped away tears. "I wish I could have been there for you, Sophie.

"I gassed up Old Blue the next morning and headed to Morton Falls. I drove with the wind in my sails, knowing that on this day, we would be reunited again. God had answered my prayers. I wasn't sure how things would go, but I wanted a chance for us. I believed that we both deserved a second chance. When I stood outside the courtroom doors and saw you walk through, I wanted nothing more than to drop to my knees and cry. I always loved you, Sophie." Her voice shook.

I leaned over to Lila and wrapped my arms around her. She pulled me in to hold me close to her heart. We both cried.

Indeed, it was a beautiful Sunday afternoon, and as we drove back to the farm, Lila and I found a new peace, a new understanding, a new truth. I needed time to digest everything she had shared. As soon as we arrived at the farm, Hunner and I jumped from Old Blue and ran to the shed as fast as our legs could carry us to gather our fishing tackle and head to the pond. I figured there was no better place to rest my thoughts. Earlier in the week, I spent several hours cleaning and organizing all the fishing tackle and garden tools in Grandpa's shed and then appropriately baptized the space as mine. With one foot out of the shed and tackle in hand, I stopped abruptly when I heard Lila yelling from the porch of the house.

"Hurry, Sophie! Hurry!" she yelled at the top of her lungs. She sounded frantic, so I dropped everything and ran to the house. Hunner followed directly behind me.

"Sophie, hurry!" she continued to yell as if the house were burning down.

When we got to the house, Hunner and I were exhausted and out of breath. To my surprise, Lila was standing on the porch with a big grin on her face. My panic was soon replaced by sheer aggravation. *What could have been so damn important to scare the hell out of me like this?*

"You have a phone call," she said excitedly as she jumped up and down on the porch, looking as if she were about to pee her pants.

"That's it?" I replied sharply. "Jesus! If you get this excited over a phone call, I wonder what you're going to do when the doorbell rings." I looked at her as if she had lost her marbles and went inside to take the call.

I was as surprised as Lila that I was receiving a phone call. It was the first time since I had arrived at the farm that anyone had called me. But seriously, it was only a phone call.

For a brief moment, fear rushed through my body. What if it was Gabe? I had foolishly given him the phone number in my first letter, and I had neglected to send the second letter, which I still had tucked between my mattresses. I was done with him.

"Hello?" I said quietly.

"Sophie?" The voice of a young man came over the phone. "Are you there?"

Recognizing his voice, I was overcome with excitement and pinched myself, hoping this wasn't a dream. My heart dropped to my feet, and butterflies took flight in my stomach; I found myself speechless. I was relieved that Gabe wasn't on the other end of the line, but the phone call was a reminder that I needed to get my letter in the mail to him. "Yes, this is Sophie," I said softly, while trying to contain the volcano of excitement ready to explode inside me.

"I was hoping that you'd go to prom with me," Blake said.

My excitement had reached a whole new level, and there were no longer words to describe how I was feeling. I realized I had never felt this way with Gabe. These feelings were foreign and more pleasurable than anything I had ever known. After a few moments, I managed to collect myself and answer. "Yes!" I replied happily.

"Cool," he said with a hint of enthusiasm. "We'll talk more at school."

Blake hung up, and I held the phone, taking in a deep breath. I closed my eyes and just felt the moment. So many thoughts were running through my mind. *Why me? Why not me?* I was elated.

Lila was still waiting on the porch, wanting to find out who had called me. She stood looking at me through the porch door with eyes as big as saucers and a smile that appeared stuck on her face.

Without further delay, I laid the receiver down.

"Was it a boy?" she said, excitement in her voice.

"No, Lila, it was Shelly, and she just has an extremely deep voice," I said. "Of course, it was a boy!" I laughed.

I could tell that with each moment I delayed, Lila found me less and less amusing. I had to tell her who was on the phone before she had a heart attack. "I'm going to the prom!" I shouted, enthusiasm bleeding from every part of my body.

I joined Lila on the porch. We took hands, and acting as if we were two little girls, we began jumping up and down. I screamed, and she screamed, and then we screamed together.

"Who's the lucky guy?" she asked impatiently.

"Blake Gerard!" I happily shouted his name.

Immediately, I realized Lila didn't share my enthusiasm. Her face appeared flushed, as if she had just heard the name of a ghost. Her expression was one that I hadn't seen before, and her reaction confused me.

"Lila, is there something wrong?" I asked carefully.

"No," she replied hesitantly. "You just caught me by surprise."

"Caught you by surprise? It appears that I've shocked the hell out of you!"

"I'm truly happy for you, Sophie," she said with a forced smile. "But supper isn't going to get cooked by itself." She retreated inside the house.

After supper, I went back to the shed and put away the fishing poles and tackle. The day had been long, and instead of going fishing, Hunner and I had sat on the porch, soaking our thoughts in the sun. If my emotions were a crayon, I could have filled a whole box. Having the answers to my mother's departure from the farm was only a small piece of the puzzle. There were more mysteries that remained.

Lila's reaction to my phone call was puzzling and heavy on my mind. My thoughts drifted back to the drive from River Crossing to Morton Falls as we passed the Gerard farm. It was a moment that had caught my attention, and I was certain Lila intentionally avoided any description or discussion of the Gerards and even appeared somewhat uncomfortable as we passed their farm. Was there a connection here? Was there a connection with the old church ladies? I would have to let this go and grant her the same peace and respect for her past as she had for mine.

Hunner and I retreated to my room for the evening. I couldn't wait to write in my journal and finish my letter to Gabe. I would mail it first thing in the morning and be free of him forever. It had been a day loaded with emotions, some that were familiar and some that were entirely new and surprising. I lay in bed looking out the window and going over every moment and detail. My prayers were to my mother on this special night, and as I talked to her, I felt as if she were sitting on the moon listening. I was angry with the choices she had made, but I still loved her. Who was I to judge when I myself had fallen far from grace. I told her how happy I was that Blake asked me to the prom. I still couldn't believe he picked me.

"Why not you?" I heard her whisper from the moon.

Exactly. Why not me? When did I let myself believe that I was less than anyone else? If I couldn't believe in myself, how could others believe in me? I wrote in my journal, *I am exactly as God intended me to be—his.* I fell asleep as Mom watched me from the moon.

Chapter 13

Work on a farm is never-ending, with something always needing to be done, and the next few weeks proved to be extremely busy. Lila and I continued with chores, and the list of repairs would keep both of us consumed for the entire summer.

"Taking care of a farm is a man's work," Lila always said. But I knew she could've outworked any man in the county. She never complained. She always said that complaining was a complete waste of energy, so she just kept going, every now and then stopping to sit by Grandpa's garden, lifting her face and thoughts to the sky. She was a quiet woman who worked hard and kept to herself.

Robert and Hilly loved to come and visit in the evenings after a long day's work. One evening, when they came over, we sat on the porch. The talk began, as usual, with conversation of work that needed to be done on the farm. Lila, always the gracious host, had prepared fresh lemonade and homemade cookies. Hilly, who was famous for her baking, brought something amazing that she had baked specially for us. She led a more active role in the community and had all the latest gossip on the townspeople, including the nasty church ladies. Although Lila normally didn't entertain gossip, you couldn't help but listen and laugh at the stories Hilly told.

"I hear Lou Lou Bell's on a diet," Hilly said, rustling her big butt into the wicker porch chair. "She's gonna eat nothin' but vegetables and fruit."

"Sounds like a healthy lifestyle to me," Lila replied.

"Sounds like several trips to the bathroom to me." Hilly laughed out loud.

"I think we should lock the doors to the bathroom at church on Sunday," I said. Imagining Lou Lou Bell running for the trees, I laughed hysterically in my mind.

"Sophie, that's not very nice," Lila said, but with a devious smile. She added, "I admit, I could stand to lose a few pounds myself."

"My mama told me that a little meat on the bones makes for a strong and healthy woman," Hilly said, sitting in a chair that was hugging her ass so tight, the seams of the wicker were about to split. "All this foolishness with trying to look like these skinny little models you see on television. A man wants something to hold on to. Isn't that right, Robert?"

"Don't drag me into this," Robert said wisely.

"Well, the next thing you know, she'll be having breast implants, then a face-lift, and before you know it, she'll be divorced and trying to steal our men," Hilly said, with a hint of sourness.

"You don't have to worry about her stealing me, cupcake," Robert said sweetly. "I only have eyes for you."

"Aw," Lila cooed.

Hilly continued on, giving a play-by-play on all the latest gossip, which kept me amused throughout the evening. Lila shook her head and pretended not to listen, even though she was soaking up every word like a sponge soaking up water. Lila said she didn't believe half of what Hilly said, but she had to admit that her stories were quite entertaining at times. In a small town like Morton Falls, the only entertainment was gossip. Too bad, it was at the expense of its own people.

The prom was quickly approaching, and I was starting to worry; shopping was limited in small towns, and I feared that I might not be able to find a dress suitable for the occasion.

As I sat on my bed one morning, writing in my journal, Lila peeked her head into my room. "What are you doing just sitting there, Sophie?" she asked, a sly smile spreading across her face. "Get dressed and hop in the truck. We've got shopping to do."

My heart leaped, and I sprang from the bed. I heard Lila giggling as she walked off down the hall. After throwing a T-shirt over my head and pulling on a pair of jeans, I slipped my feet into my sneakers and headed downstairs.

Lila was waiting at the front door, keys in hand. "Ready to go?"

"Are you kidding me?" I replied, hopping over the last three steps to the floor. "I was born ready."

Once on our way, my initial excitement waned. What if I couldn't find a dress I liked? Or one that fit right? I bit my lip and stared out the passenger side window.

A gentle hand on my knee jolted me from my thoughts. I turned and looked at Lila.

She smiled and returned her hand to the steering wheel. "We'll find the perfect dress for you, I promise."

I leaned back against the seat in relief. "Lila, how is it you can always read my thoughts?"

Entering the store, our excitement was short-lived. Inside stood two of the infamous church ladies, Lou Lou Bell Roberts and Beatrice Meyer, who appeared to be shopping for hats. Usually, the pack of wolves ran in three. We were surprised to find that the leader of the pack, Vivian Gerard, hadn't accompanied them.

The store was far too small to avoid confrontation, so Lila, in keeping with her Christian character, greeted them with her classic half smile and a kind hello. They returned the greeting with an unkind turn of the head, as if they hadn't noticed her.

"Let me at 'em, Lila," I said fiercely, with the courage of a lion.

I could see in her eyes how they had hurt her, even if she refused to admit it to me. I was hurt for her. I found myself wanting to protect her, and I didn't have nearly her patience nor her tolerance for their cruel behavior.

I began to plunge forward when Lila placed her hand around mine and squeezed gently, just as she had done in church. It was her way of reminding me to keep calm.

"What did you do to those old bats?" I whispered quietly to her.

"Not now, Sophie," she said, still squeezing my hand as we continued to check out the store for a dress.

My patience was wearing thin with these two Bible-thumping, mean-spirited bats, and Lila wasn't letting me in on her secret. There had to be a great story here, and I'd bet Hilly knew every juicy detail. Time would unlock this secret, but my curiosity was becoming unbearable.

Cautiously scanning the store, we did everything possible to avoid the evil, twisted-faced church ladies as they continued to snicker and stare. Our attention was drawn away from them when Lila held up the perfect dress. Ivory in color, it had an off-the-shoulder neckline and a floor-length hemline. The neckline was embellished with a classic palette of tiny pink and plum rosettes, giving the dress a romantic 1950s flair. Lila smiled and shared that she had the perfect necklace to match.

I put the dress on and stood in front of the mirror admiring myself.

Tears of joy slowly rolled down Lila's cheeks. She tried to contain her emotion, but it wasn't possible. She whispered through her cracked voice, "You look just like your mother."

I gave her a hug. I had never worn anything so beautiful, and I was beginning to see myself as a young woman. Slowly, the rough edges were becoming smoother with each passing day. Lila and I were both changing, or possibly, changing each other.

Leaving the store with my new dress, I reminded Lila that I couldn't wait to hear the story of the old hags.

She steadily ignored me as we walked back to Old Blue.

"Are you ever going to tell me?" I asked again, jumping into Old Blue.

"I would rather cut off my tongue," she replied sharply.

I was disappointed at the possibility that I might never know what had happened. She was keeping her secret safe.

Hunner and I continued to work Grandpa's garden. It was growing like weeds, and the weeds were growing like weeds too. My probationary period on the farm was ending soon. After Lila's report to the judge, she was granted permission to retain legal custody of me for the time being, at least until I turned eighteen, and I could remain with her on the farm. All charges against me from the robbery were dropped, and my slate was clean. God believed in me, and I in him. It was an equal and mutual exchange. I didn't realize he offered the same opportunity to everyone.

Life had become everything I had always dreamed of before Mom died. Lila reminded me often that life's most profound lessons happen in a moment, where everything is changed and nothing looks or feels the same. The soul is looking through the same set of eyes, but the depth of the soul has been forever changed. Always changing...forever...a garden growing.

Chapter 14

Each day brought a new adventure on the farm. The bus ride home from school was my fifteen minutes of rest. When I arrived home, chores came first, allowing little time for Hunner and me to play. Work was plentiful and, Lila said, necessary for the spirit. I sometimes questioned her philosophies.

My love for my garden had grown to new levels, and I was excited each time I saw a tiny sprout push through the soil reaching for the sun. Lila was happy that I had taken over the garden with such care and even more impressed that I promised to eat everything that I had planted. Robert was right when he said there is personal reward in using the land to create a bountiful harvest of food. I wasn't a huge fan of vegetables, but I hoped my taste buds would acclimate to them. Watermelons and cantaloupe would be coming in late summer, and I couldn't wait to eat something that I really liked. Lila used everything in the garden, and what we couldn't eat, she canned. Waste was not a word you used on the farm. If you couldn't eat it, can it, or recycle it, well, then you gave it to the pigs.

Nature was exploding with magnificent colors of green. The reawakening of spring ignited a personal inventory, forcing me to look inward at my own rebirth, my own spiritual baptism. I found my peace at the pond, and every evening, Hunner and I playfully splashed around, making sure to scare away any other creature that possibly inhabited the lake. Hunner and I worked on developing our own skills to communicate, and he was beginning to understand my commands, as I was beginning to understand his responses. We played a game with a toy pheasant where I would throw it into the pond and he would swim to retrieve it, bringing it back to me to do it all over again and again and again. He rarely tired. I tired long before he did.

It was another beautiful Sunday afternoon, and Robert would be celebrating his seventieth birthday. Earlier in the week, Hilly invited Lila and me to his birthday party. We looked forward to Hilly's invitations, as the food was beyond this world, and Robert's company was always refreshing, not to mention the comical skills he possessed at killing jokes. However, on Sunday morning, Hilly invited the entire church congregation, including the notorious church ladies whose entire existence depended on social gatherings to feed their appetite for gossip, not to mention their stomachs.

Although Lila didn't seem thrilled to attend, she graciously accepted the invitation. I, however, sincerely apologized for missing such a memorable event, saying my services would be better utilized tending the farm in Lila's absence. She smirked in disgust, knowing full well that I was being sarcastic and that she would rather be spending the day with me and Hunner. Hell, she would probably rather spend the day pulling her own teeth, but she loved Robert deeply and wouldn't miss his birthday just to avoid the old bats.

Grandpa's fishing tackle was packed and ready for its journey to the lake, while Hunner and I prepared a small cooler of snacks along with a jug of lemonade for a lazy afternoon of fishing. I took my time walking to the pond, treasuring every moment as I relived the memories of my first day on the farm and how the pond took my breath away. The rest of my thoughts were hijacked by Blake and the upcoming prom. I created a scenario in my mind of the night, so unbelievable it could only exist in a fairy tale, possibly setting myself up for a major disappointment.

Upon arriving at the pond, I couldn't believe the magnificent landscape. It was as if God had whispered for everything to be still. The lake had virtually become a mirror of the sky and the surrounding trees, so pristine it was almost impossible to decipher the land from the sky. I could have stood staring at its beauty forever, but Hunner had other ideas, and he disturbed the image by jumping in and playfully splashing. The waves rippled slowly across the pond, rolling gracefully until they reached the other side. There is a peace in nature that can only be felt with the soul.

Preparing my fishing pole, I baited my hook with a night crawler, known as a worm in Nebraska, and cast my line into the pond. I sat beside the old rotted log along the bank in the cool, fresh grass and watched Hunner as he splashed incessantly, scaring off any chance I had of catching a fish. Off in the distance, I noticed a mother duck and her three little ones following closely behind her. A tree along the shore of the pond accommodated several turtles sunning themselves. An old weathered tree on the other side of the pond still stood with branches broken and worn, holding the nests of several eagles. I watched as they flew in and out. Some sat silently on the dead limbs as if they were keeping guard of the nests, while others flew effortlessly amid the blue sky...another one of God's great creations.

Hunner finally retreated to the bank, and after showering me as he shook the water from his coat, he lay down to rest beside me and the old log. I rigged my pole with a bell, placed it in the pole holder, and lay down beside Hunner. We both drifted away in our thoughts. Closing my eyes, I focused on all the sounds that surrounded the pond. Frogs were loud and busy talking to one another, birds were singing a melody, and every now and then, the bell on my pole rang, triggering our excitement in anticipation of that big catch. These were special times we shared together lying quietly under the warm sun, listening to nature's lullaby, and getting lost in our dreams. I couldn't buy that kind of peace anywhere.

Suddenly in the midst of all these sounds, off in the distance, I could hear something brushing through the tall grass as if someone were walking near us. Hunner's head raised, and he began barking. We both began looking in all directions.

"Who's there?" I called out loudly.

No one answered, yet I could still hear footsteps drawing near.

"Who's there?" I yelled, louder this time.

I felt my heart beating faster wondering who was approaching. For a moment, stricken with fear at the possibility it could be Gabe, I found myself weak with panic. I had no choice but to use my last option. "Go get 'em, Hunner!" I shouted.

Hunner took off running through the tall grass, and in an instant, he was out of my sight. In the distance, I heard a young man whose voice sounded familiar.

"Call him off, Sophie," he yelled. "It's me, Blake!"

I could hear them getting near, and I could only imagine Hunner barking fiercely, following at his heels, and nipping at his ankles. I laughed to myself when I saw them nearing the bank of the pond. Blake was running with his fishing pole and tackle held high over his head, and exactly as I had imagined it, Hunner was right on his heels.

"Hunner, stop!" I yelled.

My trying to command but laughing at the same time was impossible for Hunner to understand. He finally calmed down, and Blake dropped his fishing gear to regain his composure and catch his breath.

I tried to hide any enjoyment I was experiencing at seeing Blake startled. "What are you doing here?" I asked, giggling, while keeping Hunner at bay. "You practically scared me to death."

"Just came to fish," he said politely. "I didn't realize I'd be greeted with such a warm welcome." He laughed.

"You fish?"

"I live to fish," he replied with a smile. "I've been fishing this pond as long as I can remember. My grandpa lives over there." He pointed toward the Gerard farm." He paused and looked at me with conviction. "I can even bait my own hook."

"Ha-ha," I said, laughingly.

"Do you mind if I sit here and fish with ya?" Blake asked politely.

"I think that'd be okay, if it's all right with Hunner."

With a cocked head and bewildered stare, Hunner remained aloof.

"I guess that means it's okay," I said. We looked at each other and laughed.

Blake cast his pole, and we both sat beside the old log, with Hunner at our feet. Despite the fact that Hunner had nearly assaulted him, they quickly took a liking to each other. God had finally answered one of my prayers. This was my dream of a perfect day.

"Are you excited about the prom?" Blake asked.

"Yes," I said shyly, with a smile. "Thank you for asking me."

"Thanks for accepting," he replied, also with a smile.

"I have my dress," I said excitedly. "I hope you'll like it."

"I'm sure you'll be beautiful," he said reassuringly, with sincerity in his eyes and gentleness in his voice.

For a moment, we both sat awkwardly silent and peered out at the lake, as if we didn't know what to say next.

"Why did you ask me to the prom?" I questioned carefully, still casting doubt on his invitation.

"Because I knew you'd say yes," he joked.

His response wasn't what I expected, but his playfulness was refreshing, and I bought in by pushing him over and wrestling flirtatiously as we both laughed. Finally, we came to rest upon the ground beside the old log, with Blake holding his body carefully above mine. He studied my face, and I watched him breathlessly, waiting for his lips to meet mine.

Softly brushing the hair from my face, he slowly ran his fingers down my cheeks. "Why wouldn't I ask you?" he said softly.

Removing himself from my body, he sat back up against the log and took a deep breath.

I had been foolish to ask the question and was disgusted that I had allowed myself to display my own self-doubt. Luckily, the moment was short-lived, as the tip of Blake's pole took a deep dive, sending both of us to our feet. Blake not only caught the biggest fish, he caught the only fish.

We talked the rest of the evening, and hours passed as if they were only minutes. For the first time since my mother's death, I was able to share stories of her life without tears. Blake listened sympathetically, and I found myself sometimes lost in my own words as I looked at him. He was my miracle. Miracles seemed at home here on the farm, and I embraced God and all his glory. Hands down, this was the best day of fishing I had ever had. I didn't catch a single fish, but what I wanted to catch was sitting right beside me. I hoped he was hooked.

We could have talked ourselves into the morning. We were both finding it difficult to part from one another, but with darkness upon us, we knew it was time to leave the pond. Pulling in our poles, we packed up our belongings and were ready to depart for the night. We stood looking at one another, not knowing how to say good-bye.

"I had a great day," Blake said. He took my hand and reached over to kiss me on the cheek.

I lowered my face and blushed. He made me feel like it was the first time I had ever been kissed.

"Me too," I said softly.

It was the end of a perfect day. Walking back to the farm, I thanked God for bringing Blake into my life, and I began replaying over and over in my mind the gentleness of his lips kissing my cheek.

The next few weeks were hell with the anticipation of the prom. Blake and I exchanged smiles in the hallway at school, and I sat in class daydreaming about our day of fishing, hoping that there would be more. Every part of my body was screaming for him as I tried to go on as normal as possible, but patience certainly wasn't one of my virtues, and I wanted nothing more than to sink into his body.

Time passed quickly as Lila and I worked exhaustively on fixing fencing around the farm and many other projects that were waiting for our attention. My body couldn't take much more wear and tear. My hands were already calloused from my gloves slipping as I hammered wooden stakes into the ground and held on tightly while Lila attached the fencing wire. I'd hoped the first time Blake held my hand, it would be soft, not grotesquely covered with blisters. However, Blake's family were also farmers, so I was sure he'd had more than a day or two of calloused hands himself.

Finally, the day came, and God blessed us with a beautiful Saturday morning. I was used to Rosco waking me every morning, and I would rush out of bed to breakfast, but on this particular morning, I wanted to lie in bed for a while and soak it all in. I felt like the luckiest girl in the world, and I wanted to take pleasure in every moment of the day. I still couldn't figure out why Blake had chosen me as his date, but I was no longer willing to let thoughts of insecurity consume any part of this day. Lila said God created each of us with a special gift, and it's up to us to honor him by using it. I hadn't identified what my special gift was yet, but I hoped that when I found it, Blake would be around to witness it.

I looked at my dress hanging from the closet door and imagined myself dancing in Blake's arms like Cinderella at the ball. The smell of Grandma's breakfast wafted through the house, but Hunner was warm on my feet, and my mind was free with wonderful thoughts of a night to come. We would just lie here for a while longer.

As the day progressed, both Lila and I were overcome with anxiety and excitement. She insisted on running me a bath earlier than what I had anticipated. Although I wasn't ready, I agreed because she wanted so badly to be helpful and a part of the preparation of this day. She laced the water with bath pearls, and the aroma of lilacs filled the house. Everything was exquisite. I couldn't help but want to stay in the tub for hours. The bathtub was a large old claw-foot tub, and I sank deeply into both the water and my thoughts. I closed my eyes and imagined myself lying next to the water on a white sand beach with the cool breeze floating above me. I pictured Blake lying beside me with sun-streaked hair and tanned skin accenting every part of his body. I wanted to lie forever in the moment, but the night was mine, and I needed to get ready.

Lila zipped up the back of my dress, and I stood looking into the old mirror, with her peering over my shoulder. We were both having a difficult time believing what our eyes were seeing. Lila had curled my hair and pinned it up, leaving some golden locks to fall around the back of my neck and face. The locks looked like crystals hanging from a chandelier. The ends of the pins were decorated with small pearls that Lila had placed throughout my hair like artwork. Everything looked beautiful.

"We have one last thing to add," she said.

She left the room, and my anticipation grew with each passing minute.

Upon returning, she was carrying the most beautiful necklace I had ever seen. "Sophie, this was given to me by someone very special. I would really love for you to wear it tonight, that is, if you like it." She seemed eager for me to accept.

"I love it," I said happily.

Lila gently hung the necklace made of pearls around my neck and fastened the clasp. She looked once again over my shoulder and into the mirror. "You look beautiful," she said, smiling proudly. "You'll take Blake's breath away."

That's exactly what I hoped for. When the door opened and he walked in, I would gracefully walk down the staircase. Upon our eyes meeting, I wanted him to gasp as if he had never seen anything as beautiful in his life. I wanted to take his breath away.

Lila and I took one last moment to look in the mirror. I saw a young woman whose garden of life had changed, and I loved it.

We both wanted to say something, but another speechless moment overtook us. We simply had no words.

We heard a knock at the front door, and my heart began skipping beats. I couldn't move, so Lila gently gave me a nudge.

"It's time!" she said with excitement. She proceeded down the stairs to let Blake in, and I had to pinch myself one more time to believe I was really standing there.

I was scared, but I wasn't going to turn back now. I slowly began my descent down the stairs, and at the moment Blake came into full view, my breath was taken away. I didn't notice if he was breathing or not. I was so overcome with emotion, I only wanted to make sure I was breathing. We both looked at each other differently than we had before, and it was in that moment, in one moment all alone by itself, that all of Lila's quirky messages began to come clear. It's in an instant, a moment, that our lives are transformed, forever changed. I had been given a miracle, and he was standing at the bottom of the stairs waiting for me. He stepped forward to take my hand, still not having said a word.

Lila was witnessing something she had seen and known before, and in all her joy, she merely stood silent with her hands on her cheeks.

"You are beautiful. I mean, you look beautiful," Blake said, stuttering and tripping over his words.

"Thank you," I said graciously and took his hand.

We both began to breathe as he gently placed a corsage with butter-colored carnations and white baby's breath on my wrist; it matched my dress perfectly. The touch of his hands on mine sent an array of shivers down my spine, and I almost found myself raising my hands to my cheeks like Lila, completely overwhelmed with emotion.

Blake helped me into his truck, carefully making sure my dress wouldn't get caught in the door. Within minutes, we arrived at the high school. Blake parked his truck and jumped quickly from the cab to open the door for me, another surprising first for me. I liked it.

Blake took my hand, smiling from ear to ear, and before entering the auditorium, he asked, "Are you ready for this?"

I nodded.

Stepping through the doors, we were presented in the grand march as Mr. Blake Gerard and his beautiful guest, Ms. Sophie Mae Randolph. All eyes were on us, and I truly felt like a princess.

After the grand march, Blake and I found a table closest to the corner, which allowed us a more private setting. Keeping in character as a respectful gentleman, Blake pulled my chair from the table. After seating me, he pulled his chair close to mine.

"Can I get you a drink?" he asked.

"Thank you. I mean, yes, thank you." I spoke awkwardly. I wasn't comfortable, and although I wanted to believe that I belonged here with Blake, I still had that other voice inside me doubting everything.

"I'll be right back," he said. He laughed a bit at my uneasiness. "It's okay."

Sitting alone, I felt vulnerable. I was a fake. If Blake knew who I was, what I had done, I certainly wouldn't be sitting here now. The comments I overheard only enhanced my insecurity.

"Where do you suppose she stole her dress from?" Penelope said laughingly to Tiffany only a few tables away.

"I don't think they make prom dresses with stripes," Penelope replied rudely.

"Blake seriously needs a reality check," Tiffany snipped. "He's way too good for her."

Obviously consumed with jealousy, they continued their snickering and distasteful comments, and I sat staring out into the auditorium, believing they were right. Tears began to well up in my eyes, and I lowered my head. I wanted to get up and run. Makeup was surely going to start smudging if I began crying, so I fought desperately to remain calm.

"Sophie, what's wrong?" Blake asked with concern. He placed our drinks on the table and sat down, then quickly took a napkin and dabbed the corners of my eyes to dry up the tears. "Did someone say something?"

The girls laughed loudly enough to be noticed. I saw by Blake's face that he quickly realized where the tension had come from.

"Sophie, look at me," he said gently, while lifting my chin with his hand. "You asked me at the pond why I chose you. I could see through your eyes how beautiful you are, not just on the outside, but on the inside. Your heart shines through your eyes. The first day I saw you beside my locker, I knew there was something special about you, and I wanted to be a part of whatever it was that made me feel that wonderful."

I smiled, though not yet completely convinced that I belonged there.

"I don't care what you've done or where you've been. I do know one thing: whatever it is, it has made you an incredible lady. Now, would you like to sit here at the table and cry, or would you like to dance with a hunk like me?"

I laughed despite myself.

Taking my hand, Blake led me to the dance floor. The auditorium was decorated spectacularly in silver and black. Streamers hung from every part of the ceiling, and balloons flooded the floors in colors of silver and white. The theme of the prom centered around James Bond, 007. Blake sported a black tux with a silver cummerbund and a black bow tie; he was far more handsome than James Bond.

A true gentleman, he treated me as if I were the only one in the midst of this large auditorium, and we danced as if no one else were watching. I lay my head on his shoulder and rested my body in his arms. When he gently wrapped them around me, I felt as if I were lying in a blanket of love. I closed my eyes and let myself feel as if I were aimlessly floating in the heavens. Several times, I pinched myself to make sure that I wasn't dreaming. I wasn't, and the evening was even more beautiful than I could have imagined. It was magical.

With the end of the evening near, we left the dance and drove slowly back to the farm. I wanted this night to last forever. Sitting close to Blake in the truck, I slowly began pulling the pins out of my hair to let it down; locks fell on my shoulders as each pin was pulled. Suddenly, I found myself nearing the windshield as Blake hit the brakes, stopping the truck abruptly in the middle of the country road.

"Can I kiss you?" he asked, looking as if he couldn't wait another moment.

I leaned into him, and he into me, and we kissed. It was perfect. His lips were soft and his kiss so gentle, I felt my body drowning in ecstasy. Running his hands through my hair and tilting my head back, he kissed my neck, and then moved slowly up behind my ear, sending chills up my spine. We both began panting as if we had just completed a marathon run.

Blake leaned back and dropped his head against the cab of the pickup. He took several deep breaths in an attempt to shake off temptation. I could have kissed him forever and found myself wanting to give in to temptation. Putting the truck back in gear, Blake continued speechlessly down the gravel road, resting his hand on mine.

I couldn't wait to get back to the farm to tell Lila everything about the evening, but there was also a part of me that wanted the evening to never end. As we approached the driveway, I knew Lila would be waiting up for me, and it was evident, as I could see every light in the house was on. She would want to hear every detail, and I looked forward to sharing my happiness, knowing it would be mirrored by hers.

God had presented Blake and me with an evening of the most incredible moments. There were miracles everywhere, moments where our eyes had met and thousands of stories had been told. No deception, no perception—only truth.

Chapter 15

When we arrived at the farm, Blake again proved himself a gentleman by reaching for my hand to help me step down from the truck. Holding hands, we giggled and flirted with one another as we walked slowly to the porch, making every attempt to extend our time together. Surprisingly, Lila hadn't come bolting through the front door to greet us, and Hunner, usually on the heels of anything approaching the house, was nowhere in sight.

On this unbelievable evening, nothing existed except for Blake and me. With every breath I took, I felt blissfully paralyzed as his spirit embodied me. We walked slowly, hand in hand, savoring every moment. The night sky was clear, and stars blanketed the universe, surrounding us in all their beauty. As we danced earlier, I felt as if I had been in his arms before. Everything about him was like a memory deeply embedded within my soul. It was as if we had just picked up where we had left off long ago in another time and space. In his arms, I felt like I was home. In his arms, I felt love.

We approached the porch, and there was still no evidence of Lila or Hunner. Surely, Lila would have waited up for me. My senses told me something was wrong; in fact, I was overcome with anxiety. I called for Hunner, hoping to arouse movement from within or around the house, but there was still no sign of him. I lifted my dress to ascend the stairs leading to the porch, and panic rushed through every vein of my body like a wildfire. Flowerpots that had once laced each side of the steps were smashed and strewn about. Dirt from planters covered the porch, and Lila's favorite rocking chair where she would sit in the evening was broken and scattered about.

Blake quickly took charge, as I stood frozen in fear, unable to grasp reality. Shaking uncontrollably, I was paralyzed, envisioning the worst.

"Sophie, you have to be calm," Blake whispered firmly. Placing his hands on my shoulders, he stood close to me, helping to control my fear. "Look at me," he demanded quietly, staring into my eyes. "Everything's going to be okay."

His voice was confident and strong, but nothing he could do or say at this point was going to calm my mind. I had already crossed all boundaries of sanity, and there was no turning back. I wanted so badly to believe Blake, but I sensed with every part of my being that things were anything but okay.

"Stay right here," Blake commanded. "I'm going to find Lila and Hunner."

The shivers that had consumed me only allowed me to move my head up and down in acknowledgement. I didn't utter a word.

Walking quietly down the length of the porch, Blake moved slowly until he approached the corner, where he swiftly turned, entering the east side of the porch, and was no longer in my sight. Now alone with my shattered mind, the moments of him being gone felt like an eternity. With my lips trembling and shivers electrifying every cell of my body, I couldn't stand still any longer. I began walking the length of the porch, quietly and carefully. Upon reaching the other side, I found Blake kneeling beside Lila as she lay seemingly lifeless.

"Lila!" I screamed, frantically running to her.

Blake grabbed me quickly and covered my mouth with his hand, reminding me to stay quiet.

I knelt down beside Lila and gently lifted her head into my arms. Coddling her like a baby, I began to cry. I couldn't believe what I was seeing. Her face, once beautiful and radiant, was bruised and swollen. Her gown and the porch where she lay were engulfed in blood. I gently held her head in my arms and began praying silently to God to bring her back to me. I promised him I would make every wrong that I had done right. I promised I would never doubt my love for him or his for me if he would only let her live.

Blake moved quietly to the outer wall of the porch and slowly lifted himself to observe the farm. We hadn't noticed anything unusual when we drove up to the house, other than that Hunner wasn't barking. My worst fear was that something horrible had happened to him. I couldn't bear losing him. He wasn't just my best friend; he had saved me.

"I'm going inside to call for help," Blake whispered in my ear.

"No!" I cried, tugging on his shirt, pleading with him to stay with us. "Please, Blake! Whoever did this may still be inside."

He nodded. "I'll be careful. Where will I find a phone? Is there one in the kitchen?"

I had to pause to think. My mind was swirling. "Yes," I said at last. "Next to the sink. But you can't go in there alone—"

"Sophie, we have to get help," he whispered urgently. "Whoever did this is probably long gone. I need you to stay with Lila until I get back. She needs you now more than ever."

Lila's breathing was becoming more and more shallow. She needed medical attention quickly. With my fear far outweighed by my love and concern for her, I nodded for Blake to go ahead. Within a few moments, I heard the screen door squeal, and I winced. If anyone was inside, he wouldn't have missed that. I tried not to worry about that as I sat alone in the night with Lila dying in my arms.

I could hardly bear to look at her as the blood from her nose and mouth continued to flow. I feared that whoever had done this to her might still be somewhere on the farm, and they might come back to finish what they had started. I pulled strips of soft chiffon off my dress to wipe the blood from her face. She had been severely beaten and had large wounds to her head and face.

Who could have done this to such a beautiful person? Surely, they didn't know her. Her gentle smile had all but disappeared, as her lips once so soft and small were thick and plump, covered in blood. I held her head in my arms, close to my chest, and cried, thinking that if I hadn't left her home alone tonight this might not have happened. While I was out having the time of my life, she was lying here alone dying. She was not responding, and the thought of losing her felt as if someone had shot me directly in the heart. With each breath I took, it felt as if the air were suffocating me. My chest became tighter and tighter, feeling like it was about to explode.

"Don't leave me," I cried. "Please don't die. I need you." I pleaded with her desperately. "Please don't leave me."

Tears poured from my eyes and dropped onto her face. With each tear that fell, I asked God to bring Lila back to me. I prayed as I had never prayed before. Lila had once told me the most powerful thing in the world is prayer, and up to this point, she had been right about everything else. I was so scared I even began arguing with God. "She's mine!" I said angrily, looking to the heavens. "She's all I have left. You took my mom," I yelled. "You can't have Lila too."

I took my fingers and lightly brushed the blood-soaked hair from her face and gently stroked the side of her cheeks. My tears continued to flow, and silently, I repeated over and over, *She's mine. You can't take her from me. She's mine.* Fading into sheer exhaustion, I rested my head on hers.

Moments seemed like hours, and the loneliness I felt reminded me of days that I thought were long past. Suddenly, I thought I heard Lila gurgling as if she were trying to speak. I lifted my head from hers and quickly shifted her to the side. Blood poured from her mouth, and she tried to cough in an attempt to clear her throat. She struggled for a few moments to speak, and then simply stated, "I hope you had a lovely evening."

I couldn't believe it. She was back with me, and even nearing death, her only concern was if I had a lovely evening. This gracious Lila was a true and amazing woman of God.

"It was a beautiful evening," I said with a mixture of tears and laughter, and even a bit of a smile. "It'll be all right, Grandma," I assured her. "Blake is getting help."

She smiled at me proudly. Quietly, through her pain, she said, "You must be all shook up, Sophie. You just called me Grandma." Her eyes welled up with tears. "It's okay, Sophie. They're tears of joy. I've waited a long time to be called Grandma." She smiled.

"What happened here, Lila?" I asked desperately. "Who did this to you?"

Before Lila could answer, she slipped back into unconsciousness. I was afraid she wouldn't come back to me.

Blake had been gone for what seemed like forever. I trembled, wondering if something had happened to him. I was also worried sick about Lila. I didn't know how severe her injuries were, and not knowing what had happened haunted my every thought. My patience was surely being tested as I sat with her. *Who could do this to her?* I wondered. *Who could be so cruel?*

Lila drifted in and out of consciousness. I gazed into her eyes, and I could see my mom lying in my arms. I felt her lifeless body. Words can never describe the pain I felt the night Mom passed away. I was numb. Everything in my body and my mind shut down, until, well...until the farm.

Where is Blake? I thought. *Why hasn't he come back to us?* I needed to get Lila help right away. I had lost all track of time and had no idea how long I had been waiting on the porch. What I did know was that time was passing, and every moment was a moment closer to Lila's death. My patience was wearing thin, and I just couldn't wait any longer. Lila came to for a brief moment.

"Lila," I said softly. "Please stay awake. I need to leave you and go get help."

"Go," she said, and reaching for my hand, she held it tightly. "Be careful, Sophie. He might still be here." Lila's hand loosened as she drifted back into unconsciousness.

"Wait, Lila, wait! Please stay awake. Who's here? Who did this to you?"

With no reply, I knew I had to find Blake and get help. I was now concerned for his safety as he hadn't returned and I still hadn't seen or heard Hunner.

I slowly tiptoed across the porch, peering in each window of the house. Several lights were on inside, but I couldn't make anything out through the curtains, and there was no movement within the house. I quickly darted across the porch and approached the front door. In the moonlight, I could see that Blake's truck was still there. I was overwhelmed with fear and began yelling for Blake and Hunner. I waited a few more moments for a response, but to no avail.

Turning to leave the porch, I was startled when the front door screeched and slammed behind me. In the stillness of the night, the sound was so intense I jumped and left my heart at my feet. Standing before me in the present was the past. It had returned with a vengeance. Its name was Gabe.

Chapter 16

In front of me, evil had taken its place like an old friend. When I looked at Gabe, his eyes were filled with fire and an expression of rage that I had seen too many times before. This time, however, my reaction was different. Though fear tried to take hold, my will to help Lila was far stronger than my fear of Gabe. I wasn't going to cower before him.

Visibly drunk, he swayed from side to side on the porch, slipping every so often in the dirt from the flowerpots. He waved a bottle of vodka in one hand and a cigarette in the other. Prison hadn't been good to Gabe by the looks of him. Once sporting a robust physique, he now appeared weak and thin and smelled of days' old body odor. Regardless of how he looked, I wasn't quick to forget the state of his dangerous mind.

"Are you Little Red Riding Hood?" he asked, slurring his words. "'Cause I'm the big bad wolf, and I've come to eat your grandma." He growled and then laughed eerily.

When he moved closer to me, I could feel his breath on my face and smell the stench of cigarettes that permeated his clothing.

"Cat got your tongue?" he scoffed with a smile, taking pleasure in my fear as I stood frozen in silence.

"I'm just surprised to see you," I replied quietly. The words shook from my mouth.

"I'll bet you're surprised," he said with a smirk. Flicking his cigarette butt on the porch, he set his bottle down, grabbed my neck, and began squeezing.

Rage that I had never felt before began stirring in every corner of my mind and body. I wanted to kill him for what he had done to Lila, and if I couldn't succeed in saving her, I *would* kill him. "Gabe!" I shouted. I grabbed his hand and removed it from my neck. "What are you doing?" Turning my tone to butter, I said, "I've been waiting for you to come for me for months. What took you so long, baby?" I hoped he would find my act believable. I wasn't much of an actress, but I wasn't vying for an Oscar; I was vying for our lives.

Gabe stumbled back away from me. He remained aloof, blatantly ignoring my affection.

It became evident I was in real danger.

"Who's the little boy?" he asked irritably, with a sneer on his face.

"Oh, you mean Blake?" I played it off stupidly. "He's just some church boy the old lady I'm staying with made me escort to the school dance. He doesn't mean anything to me." I reached out to Gabe.

He took my hand and pulled me violently into his body. Wrapping his arms tightly around me, he pushed his lips into mine and began kissing me. The taste of his mouth mixed with vodka and cigarettes nauseated me. Before pulling away, he intentionally bit my lip, causing it to bleed.

I continued groping him, hoping he would buy into my game. "I can't wait to get out of here," I whispered seductively in his ear. "You can't imagine the hell I've been through, baby. But it's over now, right? Let's get out of here." I pleaded with him, hoping he would take the bait.

"What's the hurry?" he replied, smiling creepily. "I'm gonna stick around and have some fun. I've been sitting in prison for months, while you've been playing Little Orphan Annie. Look at these digs." He picked up his bottle and waved it toward the house. "Wearing fine clothes and living like a princess. You must really think you're something."

"Gabe, I swear, I've been waiting for you," I whispered, rubbing his neck. "Why do you think I wrote you? I begged you to come for me." I ran my tongue around his ear.

Still cold and detached, Gabe didn't return my affection. I persisted in my attempt to win him over, but his rejection left me feeling desperate.

"Yeah, I got your letter." He laughed under his breath. Pulling another letter from his back pocket, he shoved it into my chest. "And I got this one from your room."

I stood before him silent. I had never gotten around to mailing the second letter and had left it on the writing desk in my room. How could I have been so stupid? The letter was my good-bye to Gabe.

"Cat got your tongue again?" he asked, parading around me studying my fear, as well as my defeat.

"Gabe, listen to me," I pleaded. "You can have a different life than the one we used to live. I know, because I'm a testament to how people can change. You're a good person, Gabe. You took care of your little brother when no one else would. I didn't like it when I first got here, and I had no idea that I even had a grandmother, but now that I do, I love her. I can't lose her, Gabe. Please let me help her." I hoped to strike the last bit of sensibility Gabe had left.

Reminded of his brother, he lowered his head and maintained a somber silence.

"I know prison isn't the life you want. Life can be good for you. I can help you, Gabe. But I can't help you if you're in prison for murder. Lila is hurt badly, and I don't know what you've done to Blake."

"He won't be going anywhere for a while," Gabe confessed. His voice was becoming tired, and he seemed to be irritated as he began pacing back and forth across the porch, every so often lifting the bottle of vodka to pour down his throat. "He had an accident." He laughed to show his amusement. "You really should pick 'em better, Sophie. Didn't I teach you anything?"

"Gabe, please," I begged. "I can help you."

"You don't fool me!" he snapped. His fist met my face, knocking me clean off my feet. He grabbed my hair and pulled me into the house.

I fought back, covering my face and body while he continued hitting me.

"Where's the liquor?" he shouted, laughing as he pulled harder and harder on my hair. "Cute little curls you have, my dear," he said with a snarl. Reaching into his pocket, he pulled out a knife, and with a fast sweep, he cut off a large handful of hair.

I tried to fight, but every time I reached for him or defended myself from the knife, he cut my hands and arms. "Please stop!" I screamed. "I want to live! Please, I want to live!"

"You're going to pay!" he yelled. "Nobody betrays me."

I cried and began praying as he grabbed another handful of my hair and swung me into the wall, knocking me unconscious.

When I came to, he was dragging me across the porch by my hair. Lifting me from the porch, he threw me on top of Lila. "That's what a pile of crap looks like," he said, laughing to himself.

I couldn't tell if Lila was still breathing. I hoped if she had died, that I would die along with her. Blood poured from my head, and combined with the darkness of the night, made it impossible to see anything surrounding me. Extreme pain enveloped every part of my body. Hoping Gabe wouldn't notice that I had regained consciousness, I didn't make a sound. He finally retreated into the house. I waited a few minutes before rolling down alongside of Lila.

"Sophie," Lila said softly. "Hold on, dear, it's going to be okay."

I was relieved that she was still alive, and her voice comforted me. She sounded like an angel.

"Pray with me," she said. Lila prayed to Michael, the archangel, asking him to protect us, and although her words were streaming beautifully from her mouth, I couldn't make much out of what she was saying.

"Stay awake," Lila said, shaking me as we lay on the porch. "You need to stay awake."

It was already late into the night, possibly far past midnight. Both Lila and I were badly beaten. My dress was torn and bloody. I reached to feel if the necklace that Lila had given me was still around my neck and sighed with relief to find it there. I didn't know what it meant to Lila, but what I did know was that it was very special to her. Slowly and painfully, I raised both arms and released the clasp of the necklace, taking it off and tucking it under one of the broken flowerpots. Gabe was not going to take this from either me or Lila.

I lay resting for a few minutes in sadness, wondering what had happened to Hunner. I knew that he would have done anything to protect me or Lila. I was certain Gabe would have killed him if he felt threatened. My guilt was overwhelming as I thought about how Lila and Hunner had been hurt because of me. If I hadn't come to the farm, none of this would be happening. The thought of what I had brought upon them was unbearable, and the pain I felt in my heart was excruciating.

"I'm so sorry," I cried. "I'm so deeply sorry. I was so stupid, Lila. I sent Gabe a letter several months ago with directions to your house. He wouldn't have even known where I was if I hadn't sent that letter. This is all my fault."

"It's okay, Sophie. It's not your fault," Lila said with conviction. She looked at me, her lips swollen and her face battered and bruised. Clearing her throat, she began talking through her pain, her voice shaky. "I have a story. I think you're mature enough to understand, and it will definitely clear up any curiosity you have about the church ladies." She started to chuckle, but coughed instead.

I had been waiting for this moment, but in my wildest dreams I would have never foreseen that it would be under these circumstances.

"We may not have till tomorrow, so I think it's time," she said, shifting to make herself more comfortable beside me as we lay together on the porch.

I couldn't have imagined how profound her words truly were or the significance of the messages that would last a lifetime. Lila's story would not only touch my heart, it would change everything I thought I knew with an awakening of truth that had been asleep far too long.

When we began the day anticipating the evening to come, we never envisioned the events that would lead us to the darkness of this porch. I was certainly no stranger to surprises, but the biggest surprise of all was yet to come. Hearts would be opened, secrets revealed, and there would be an awakening of our spirits in a way that we never dreamed possible.

Lila peacefully opened the door of her heart, and the words began to spill out as if she had been waiting to tell this story all of her life. It became a night to remember.

Chapter 17

The full moon shining onto the porch caressed Lila's face, its light allowing me to see her true beauty. She looked like an angel. We both had to laugh a bit as we grunted with every little move we made. Our bodies may have been broken, but our spirit was still strong and untouched.

I hadn't seen Gabe since he left me with Lila, and although I wanted Lila to believe I was okay, I was still overcome with fear knowing that he was near. No one knew better than I how violent Gabe could be. There was an evil that lived inside of him far worse than I would have expected when I first met him, and what he was capable of scared me to death. There was a fine line I would have to walk between reality and insanity with Gabe if he showed up again on the porch.

"Lila, I don't know where Gabe went," I whispered quietly. "I need to see if I can see any sign of him." I slid across the porch to the window. The lace curtains were too thick to see clearly, but I could make out a silhouette of his body sitting in Lila's chair in her favorite room where she kept all her treasures. Not sure whether he was awake or passed out, I slid back close to Lila. "He's still here," I whispered. "Go on with your story."

"Sophie, your curiosity about the church ladies didn't go unnoticed. Many times, I wanted to explain. I felt you had a right to know who I really am, but I wanted to wait for the right time to tell you. I wanted you to be old enough, or at least wise enough, to understand." She spoke genuinely. "I think it's time for you to know the whole story." Lila continued as her breath allowed, sometimes slowly and at other times as quickly as she could expel the words. "It was the spring of 1985," she said. "You would have been four years old, and I could only imagine what you looked like. I pictured a precious little girl with golden locks of hair falling down her back, a bright smile, and a heart as big as life. You were as close to my heart as if you were standing right before me. I could feel your spirit as if you were already playing and dancing on the farm. I had faith in God that he would bring you home to me. Just knowing that made the days easier."

A night of terror and pain seemed to drift away as the memories of Lila's past stepped forward. Nothing else existed in the moment except for Lila, me, and her story. Although Gabe was still near, Lila kept me intrigued and my mind away from the pain that consumed my body and the fear that consumed my spirit.

"I missed both Joe and Gracie and everything about them," she said softly, looking at the moon. "But most of all, I missed love. I know it might sound a little corny, but I missed loving someone and someone loving me back. In the evenings on hot summer nights, I would lie in a cool bath dreaming about what it would feel like to be in love again. I would fantasize about being in the warmth of a man's arms and resting my body in his. I may not have been a beautiful young girl like you, Sophie, but I hadn't given up on love. It had been a long time since your grandpa's passing. My body and spirit were starving for affection." Lila's voice was weak, and she spoke slowly, looking toward the night sky.

I encouraged her to go on.

"Robert and Hilly had helped me on the farm since Joe had been gone, but outside of their company and my social hour at church, I was alone. Every now and then, Robert would hire a farmhand to help us out. Of course, he took pleasure in hiring the strongest and most robust young men, not to mention damn good-looking ones. Sometimes, I would stand in the distance watching their sun-bronzed bodies dripping in sweat, every muscle protruding with each lift of the rake. It was like getting dessert after a long day of hard work." She laughed.

I laughed with her and smiled, knowing that with every word she spoke, a chapter in her heart was being opened and truth was setting her free.

"I was a widow," she said, "and pretty easy on the eyes. After Joe's death, the ladies at church treated me as if I were a leper. They stared and whispered as if I didn't notice. Though I was uncomfortable at times, I held my head high and sat without judgment, just as the Lord would have wanted. I have to admit, I was a bit of a rascal at times." She chuckled. "On occasion, I gave their husbands a wink just to see the ladies squirm. You would have thought I had ripped my shirt off, the way they reacted."

Listening to Lila talk about the feistier side of her personality, I realized how alike we really were.

"Spring was always a tough and busy time on the farm, but the spring of 1985 brought with it many unforeseen challenges as Robert Taylor fell ill. He was diagnosed with pneumonia and bedridden for most of the season. I had always depended on Robert to help me with the farm, and now I was tending to both of ours without any help and falling well behind. Hilly's health wasn't any better, and she needed to stay with Robert. Besides, she would have caused me a great deal more stress than she ever could have helped as she had never lifted a pitchfork in her life and was far too chubby to climb onto a tractor."

I giggled, and Lila joined in.

"I had been working sunup to sundown, and my exhaustion left me unable to think rationally. My emotions got the best of me one evening, and as I stepped down from the tractor, I fell to the ground and prayed for help. Well, you would have to have been there yourself to witness the miracle. The very next day, I received a visit from neighboring Charles Gerard. And yes, if you're wondering, Sophie, that would be the name you saw on the box of ornaments. Charles is Blake's grandfather." She gave me her half smile.

I knew there had to be some connection because of the name.

"He spoke softly as he stood before me," Lila continued. "I believed God had sent him himself. His voice was gentle, and he kindly offered to help with the crops. I didn't know much about Mr. Gerard personally, other than what I saw at church on Sundays. His wife and sons always attended the service, and they appeared to be a happy family. I had to admit, though, his wife, Vivian, acted pretty high and mighty. She was polished from head to toe with coordinating hat, dress, purse, and shoes, flawless makeup, and hands softer than a baby's butt. You could tell she never worked a day in her life." Lila almost sounded envious.

"Ha!" I gasped. "Is this the infamous Bible-thumping, better-than-everybody else, church-sinning hypocrite?" I asked, trying to contain my distain.

Lila nodded in confirmation. "The one and only."

"Oh my God! This story is riper than a tomato in late September," I replied, signaling Lila to continue.

"'Ms. Randolph,' he said graciously, 'I understand you may be in need of some help getting the crops in.' He paused for a moment of silence, took off his hat, and standing before me humbly, continued. 'I know you're not a charity case, but there are even times when I need help. I'm your man.' He smiled. 'Now, let's talk about what we need to get done.'

"I smiled," Lila said, "and a sound of relief escaped my lips as I put my hands to my face and thanked him.

"'I'll see you tomorrow morning, ma'am,' he said, and left.

"For a moment, I thought he was God himself," Lila said. "The next morning, he arrived early, just as the sun was coming up. I was busy getting machinery ready when he appeared in the barn.

"'I'll plant the beans on the north forty, and we'll meet back at the barn after that,' he said.

"When he took my hand to help lift me to the tractor, something unexpected happened. The warmth of his heart ran through every particle of his body, and his touch sent a massive eruption of shivers through mine. I looked at him as if I were holding the hand of someone I had known forever. I didn't want to let go. I'm sure for him, that was quite awkward." Recalling the memory, Lila giggled. "As he walked away, he looked back in bewilderment, almost confusion, or maybe he was just plain scared of me. I don't know. Maybe he felt it too." Lila stopped for a moment, breathing in the cool night air.

I wanted her to get on with it.

Her breath was short, but she continued, determined to tell her story. "As noon approached, I offered to make some lunch for the both of us. Charles thanked me graciously, and we agreed to meet by the big oak tree beside the house. It was a perfect place, as the spring grass was cool and soft, and the old oak trees canopied the ground with cool shade. I made a simple lunch of bologna, fruit, and freshly squeezed lemonade. I found myself monopolizing the conversation as he was quiet. He didn't seem bored, but listened intently, as if to hold on to every word I spoke. His company was refreshing.

"'Has it been hard, I mean, since Joe died?' Charles asked reservedly.

"'The farm has been hard,' I replied.

"'I never see anyone here. Do you have friends or family around the area?' he asked, as if genuinely concerned.

"'I prefer to be alone,' I responded somewhat sarcastically. 'Oh sure, I could ask the ladies from church over to tea, but I appreciate stimulating conversation, not who's stimulating who.' We both chuckled and smiled at each other in agreement.

"Sophie, it was amazing. I felt as if I were a little girl again. As the days went by, we joked with one another and played like children on God's playground. We acted as if there was nothing but the day and the two of us, nothing else existed in this space.

"I childishly threw a pitchfork full of straw on his head and then jumped hysterically as he vigorously climbed the ladder to seek revenge. We began throwing straw at one another, screaming and laughing, with straw sticking out of our hair and clothing. I was silly like a schoolgirl, and he was a giddy little boy, and for a moment in time, we were as free as the wind that carried us carelessly through the day. We laughed as if we hadn't laughed in years and fell to the barn floor rolling around, foolishly flirting with one another. Charles grabbed my waist. We turned toward one another, and our eyes spoke endless words of love." Lila took a deep breath before continuing.

I looked at her encouragingly but didn't interrupt.

"One day, I was hanging the sheets on the line, and suddenly, they looked different than they ever had before. The old clothesline wire was drooping and the wooden posts rotting, yet the corners of the sheets snapped in the wind, and the breeze lifted them into the air as if they were dancing to the rhythm of my heart. I stood in the yard with my feet firmly entrenched in the soil, taking in each breath as if it could be my last. The sun shone down upon me, and I felt the rays bleeding through my body. Raising my hands to the sky, I could feel the energy of the universe, and I felt young again. I felt like dancing. I felt love. Everything was magnified, and my senses were stronger than ever. There are many things we can expect, Sophie, but the most important changes are those that are unexpected. They will become the most profound. They will bring life to you."

Lila began coughing, and all too soon, the seriousness of our situation came flooding back with a vengeance. I rolled her to her side, and she began spitting up blood. I wiped her mouth with the skirt of my dress. The night was still, and the only sounds occupying the porch were that of the farm cats frolicking about and the screeching sound of the old porch swing as the occasional breeze gently rocked it. The air was chilly, and neither of us was dressed for an evening on the porch. I was still in my once-beautiful prom dress, and Lila had on a long pajama gown. After her coughing spell, we cuddled closely together, and I caressed her face and arms as she drifted off to sleep. Listening to her as she slowly unraveled the chains from her heart to expose every raw truth of her life was fascinating. I felt blessed to be the recipient.

I don't know how long Lila slept, but after a time, she slowly opened her eyes. "Where did I leave off?" she asked.

"You don't have to continue, Lila," I said. "You need your rest."

"But I want to go on," she insisted. "Oh yes, I remember now. We were going to the fields. Planting would be done in a few days, and Charles would have to return to his life and I to mine." She spoke sadly, knowing that their time was coming to an end. "I found several odd jobs around the house just to keep him on longer. The big house was old, and many repairs had been put on hold since Joe had died. Charles was an accomplished carpenter, and I took advantage of his skills by asking him to replace the staircase banister. It was incredible watching him work with his hands, almost arousing. He moved his hands across the wood as if he were caressing my body. I watched him carefully build the most exquisite staircase I had ever seen. Every time I walked up the steps, I ran my hands along the banister as if I was caressing his back. It wasn't just a staircase, it was a beautiful piece of art, and it was built from his heart.

"In the short time we were together, I felt alive again. I had finally found someone, and he was married." The irony in her voice said it all. "There was an undeniable energy in the air when we were in each other's presence. We felt it with every part of our being and suppressed it as if we were trying to stuff a wild elephant inside a small box. I placed my feelings in that box and put it on a shelf in my mind...hoping...praying...to keep it contained.

"We finished the planting late one evening, and both of us returned to the house dirty and tired. A sense of loss was upon us, and we were both very quiet. For days, we had talked endlessly, but that evening, well, we just couldn't find the words to say anything. I went to the kitchen to wash up, and as I heard the screen door shut behind me, there he was before me. I knew the moment I looked into his eyes that I had dreamed of this moment all of my life. Now, with him standing within a few feet of me, I felt as if my breath had been taken away. Everything I wanted to say was lost, and the only thing I had left was an honest heart beating profusely. I could feel my cheeks flush as I stood silent before him.

"He looked into my eyes, and placing his finger on my lips, he said that I needn't say anything at all, that he had dreamed of me too. For a moment, our silence became a beautiful dance, and time was nonexistent. It was as if we could talk without speaking, feel without touching, and breathe for one another.

"I lowered my eyes as he drew near to hide the sadness in my heart. How could he know what I had survived, what scars were left behind, what pains I had suffered? Would he still look at me the same? Could he love me with all that he imagined instead of what was real? I felt sad because I thought that he couldn't.

"He gently lifted my face to expose all the truth behind my eyes. Blue in color, they still sparkled, and I could sense that what he saw was not only what he had imagined—it was more. The energy running from his fingertips as he gently moved them up and down my cheek unleashed a huge wave of feelings inside of me that I hadn't known for many years. I had felt this moment in my dreams, and I had prayed that one day his arms would hold me tight. Now before me, I knew this was the man who would be my great love, my best friend. God had blessed me with a gift far beyond my dreams, and my spirit bathed in all the emotions of his touch. Love doesn't come when we're ready, and sometimes, it doesn't come even when we need it the most. It comes when it's true, and time has no place in the framework of our lives.

"Sophie, close your eyes and pray that love will touch you, and it will, when it's true." A long sigh escaped Lila's lips before she continued. "We stood silently in the kitchen, and it felt as if we were no longer of this world, but a part of the universe where only the purest of love exists. We had been given a blessed day. I wiped my hands gently on my apron, never once losing sight of his eyes.

"Charles stood for a moment, looking as if he would die if he couldn't have me. He drew toward me and I toward him. He gently began kissing my neck with the passion of a raging fire, and I threw my shoulders and head back welcoming him into my body. His hands laced up and down my back, and I wrapped my leg around him, pulling my body into his. He stopped to look into my eyes, and on that day, our first kiss, on our perfectly moistened lips, lasted for an eternity. Neither of us knew where we had gone, where we had escaped to, but it was magical, and we were ready to ravish each other's body as if we had thirsted for one another forever.

"I closed my eyes and felt him lifting me gently. I lay my head down near his chest, knowing that soon we would be lying in each other's arms. He carried me gently up the stairs to the bedroom and laid me softly on my old iron bed.

"'Come away with me,' I whispered to him.

"He reached over and turned off the light on the nightstand. I let all the weight of his body melt into mine. The moon shone from the window above, and the light poured in as if it were bathing us in its glow. He pulled me closer, and my head tilted back in the pillows as he studied me.

"'Every shadow of your face, every petal of softness in your skin is recorded in my mind,' Charles whispered in my ear. 'I want to consume you, all of you, but I want this to last forever.' His breathing became more and more desperate.

"His touch was erotic and sensuous, rapturous and inviting. I could no longer wait as I pulled him closer and closer into my skin. It had become far too electrifying, the intensity building to a state of ecstasy, and we lay within one another. He had taken me away.

"The rain began to fall against the windows as we lay side by side in our breathless exhaustion. The glow of the burning candles remained, and the memories of the night lay safely within the flames of our hearts. I had been taken away in his desires, and he was taken away in my scent. This night was a gift to each other. Our souls had become one, and we were now forever as much a part of one another as we were of ourselves. It was an amazing night, where everything in the world was put on hold, and all that existed was two people in love. 'Come away with me' was all I said." Tears poured from Lila's eyes and ran down her cheeks as the memory came pouring back into her mind.

I tried to comfort her. "Lila, you don't have to go on."

"I'll rest for a bit," she said, closing her eyes.

My body ached, and I felt my lips and eyes swelling. Surely, Gabe would eventually fall asleep or pass out. Every now and then, I heard rustling from inside the house, but I was afraid to go near the window for fear that he might see me. Pushing myself up against the wall of the porch, I pulled Lila close to me and rested her head in my lap. She was as stubborn as a mule and had insisted on telling her story despite her weariness and her shallow breathing.

I was captivated and couldn't wait to hear more. Sitting along the wall, I began reliving memories of the night before Blake and I had returned to the farm. I smiled, remembering how kind he was to me at the table when he saw me crying and how he gently wiped the tears from my eyes. He has a spirit much like Lila had described in Charles.

A loud crashing sound came from within the house. Lila started and woke quickly from her rest. "What was that?" she asked, shaken.

"Shhh!" I signaled for Lila to remain still, and we both sat frozen, careful not to make a sound. "It sounded like a window shattered," I whispered, alarmed.

Looking around the porch, I tried to find anything I could use for a weapon in the event there would be another confrontation with Gabe. Pieces of flowerpots were broken and strewn about. A few pieces were sharp enough to pierce through a person's skin. I lifted Lila's head from my lap and crawled to pick up the pieces. Quietly, I moved backed to the wall and placed them under my dress. Lila rested her head back in my lap, and we prayed. Several minutes passed with no activity from within the house. My mind was going crazy, wondering what the sound was that we had heard.

"I'm going to crawl to the front of the porch and look through the front windows," I whispered softly, again lifting Lila's head from my lap.

"Sophie, be careful," she whispered back. She held my arm firmly, afraid to let me go.

"I'll be okay," I replied. I moved slowly, dragging myself along until I reached the front of the porch. The vodka bottle that Gabe had in his possession earlier was now lying there, and glass from the window had shattered all over the wood. I couldn't see clearly through the windows, but I heard Gabe breathing heavily, and I could see his silhouette.

Slowly, I pulled myself back to Lila and rested for a minute while trying to ease my pain. "He threw the bottle of vodka through the window," I informed her quietly. "I'm sure he's still awake." Replacing the sharp pieces of pottery beneath me, I leaned back against the porch wall and raised Lila's head, resting her in my lap. I needed Lila to continue with her story. It was mesmerizing, and it kept my mind off the danger, allowing me to keep my wits about me. "Go on with your story, Lila," I said, hoping she would have the strength to continue.

Lila continued, even though she was finding it more difficult to stay awake. "Well, Charles fell asleep, and I lay next to him, watching him sleep. I studied everything about him. He was lying naked on his back with his arms resting on his chest, unaware that my eyes were tracing every part of his being. I had never looked at a man like this before. I listened to every breath that he took. I softly placed my hand on his thigh, just to feel him next to me. Nothing or no one else existed in those moments.

"As I lay naked next to him, silently in my mind, I was reliving and recapturing every touch, an excitement that I never wanted to end. I couldn't resist pulling my body closer to his, and he awakened briefly and rolled toward me. He placed his arms around me, and with a gentle kiss upon my lips, he whispered that he loved me. Then as quickly as he woke, he fell back to sleep. I wondered if he was dreaming and not aware of what he had just said. Or was it true?

"For the first time in my life, I realized that I had never known a love like this before, and my heart sank with sadness. The very thought of what I had captured left me with a feeling that I had been starved for many years. Secure in each other's embrace, we drifted off to sleep. I had rested my soul upon his and he upon mine."

Lila's words melted around her, and the pain inflicted on her body seemed nonexistent as she relived the memories of this love.

I was blown away. This story was far better than anything I had anticipated, and as I listened, my heart opened. It opened to her, to my mother, to my grandfather, to Charles, and most importantly...to love.

Chapter 18

The cool, damp air rolled across the porch like waves rolling upon a beach. I stroked Lila's face as I watched her every breath and pulled her body as close as I could into mine to keep her warm. I found myself drifting off to sleep and then immediately catching myself, knowing that I had to stay awake and keep watch over her. Slowly, her eyes opened, and she greeted me with her half smile. After taking a few minutes to remember where she left off, she continued her story.

"Charles left early in the morning, and I lay in bed staring at the chipped paint on the old farmhouse walls, dreaming of his touch. I could feel the strength in his legs and his muscular thighs as he wrapped them around me. I felt his hands softly caress my breasts and his lips warm and moist on my body. Lying alone, I wondered if I could ever again capture the magic of the night before. Sunday mornings had never felt like this, and I couldn't even imagine what my conversation would be with the Lord today at church.

"How could I have known what was going to happen? How could I have given in so easily? What would Charles think of me today? How could I face him at church and witness him run his loving hands across the small of his wife's back? It would surely be too painful to watch. The hands that had so softly swept across my body the night before would now be touching another woman. For a moment, I almost forgot that I was the other woman. The thought was so unbearable I chose not to attend the Sunday morning service.

"I pondered long and finally decided to call Hilly and tell her I wasn't feeling well and was possibly coming down with something. That would be believable, as many of the ladies in her quilting social had been ill recently. I begged the Lord for forgiveness, but still I couldn't bear pulling myself from the bed that Charles and I had shared together. Yesterday, it was just an old metal bed with mattresses worn, and today, well, a sanctuary that I would let no one else violate. It held the memories, the smells, the moments that had changed me, the moments that had transformed me into a woman I had lost long ago, so long ago I had forgotten who I was.

"I could barely close my eyes, as visions of him lay heavy on my mind. I could see and feel him hovering over my body, staring lovingly into my eyes, making love to me in every sense: with his body, with his mind, and with his soul. There was no way I could bear seeing him in person, it was too soon.

"The morning was beautiful, and as time passed, I lay in my bed, rehearsing the dream over and over. I stopped every so often to push my face down into the pillow to smell the scent that remained. I hesitated to move away from the bed, as my eyes remained drawn to the indentation of the mattress where our bodies lay together.

"I finally gained enough nerve to call Hilly, though when I picked up the phone, I still questioned whether or not I would be believable. I already felt my throat constricting and was sure my voice would break up. I had never been very good at not telling the truth. I considered myself a woman of God, a woman of integrity, faith, and honesty. In one evening, the very being of who I thought I was had been overshadowed by a power far beyond my control, and I loved that.

"I filled my day with miniscule tasks to help keep my mind busy. Every thought that entered into my mind was of Charles, and what should have been a day filled with pleasure and delight seemed utterly painful. I lowered the shades and dimmed the lights. I found myself reveling in my newfound love, but the confusion of it all left me wanting to be alone. The phone rang many times, and with each ring, I became more frustrated. I could only assume that Hilly's social promiscuity meant she had entered into too much conversation at the church social, and that my so-called illness had been more than overexaggerated. I ignored the phone and continued on with my daily routine.

"Although the day had been painful, I could only imagine that the evening would be far worse. It was only the night before that Charles had walked into my kitchen and hung his hat on the hook by the door. I relived the night all over again. I remembered that he was intent on what he wanted and what he needed, and with one look, I knew why he had finally come. We didn't have to exchange any words as we looked at each other from across the room. As the evening sun was setting, the last of the sun's rays shone through the kitchen window reflecting on his face. I was overwhelmed as I studied the shadows of his cheekbones. He was a man, solid and strong. His thick dirty-blond hair darkened a bit with dirt from the fields. His arms were solid, and as I moved my eyes up and down his body, I noticed the curves of his arms and wanted to feel his biceps.

"I found that reminiscing brought me back to the moment, and I became warm all over again, a rush that held my body under arrest and apprehended every part of the sensual woman that I truly was."

Listening to Lila, I observed the glow on her face as she talked of Charles. The whole time I had been on the farm, I had never seen her look, act, or talk with such a presence of love. It really did feel like God was near, and the peace and serenity on the porch was something I had never felt in my life. I prayed to God to let her finish her story. If she didn't, the curiosity would kill me.

"I survived Sunday, and Saturday seemed a dream away," she said sadly. "I couldn't allow myself to go through another day daydreaming with work on the farm waiting for me, and I was beginning to feel foolish throwing my thoughts into a fantasy and freezing my state of mind. Every day on the farm was a new challenge, and there was never enough time to get everything done. Just as the days kept rolling in one after the other, so did the endless list, and it was never at the mercy of a soul's emotions.

"I longed for every part of Charles: his gentle touch, his voice as soft as butter, his breath upon my neck. Unfortunately, I knew he wasn't mine. Nonetheless, it didn't change how much I wanted him. There were many evenings that, as I sat on the porch, I would see the dust trail from Charles's old pickup as he traveled down the old country road. He would slow to a crawling pace upon reaching the end of my driveway. What was he thinking as he sat looking at the porch where he first offered his hand to help or at the window where we lay looking out after a beautiful night of exhaustion wrapped in the love of each other's bodies?

"I wanted to run to him. Desperately, I wanted to tell him, 'I'm yours, Charles! I'm yours.' If he could hear me, my heart was screaming, 'Take me with you, I beg of you! Please come back to me. Can you hear me? Please hear me. Don't give up on me. You are the beating of my heart. Oh, I hurt so! Please come to me. Come away with me.'" Lila spoke with such emotion, it appeared as if she were truly reliving the moment. She rested peacefully for a short while and woke ready to continue. "The days passed, and we were approaching another Sunday service. I surely couldn't be absent again as I knew suspicions were growing. Delaying another Sunday would only solidify that something was wrong. I was going to have to find the strength inside myself to stand and face the consequences of my choices. Knowing full well that I wouldn't have changed a thing calmed my apprehensions.

"It had been a few weeks since I last saw Charles, and my mind was adrift with unanswered questions as I started speculating about why he hadn't come back to the farm, even to say a mere hello. I began wondering if I hadn't created something far more profound in my mind than what truly existed. Had I over-imagined the pleasure and delight only because I desired it so desperately? I wanted nothing more than to believe otherwise.

"I missed Charles more than I could have ever thought possible. To my delight and surprise, I found solitude and peace in music through this reflective time. Every word of every love song felt as if it had been written specifically for me, and I found myself dancing and singing again. At nighttime, I would lie in the bed where we made love and meditate to the sounds of nature. The memory of the rhythm of our bodies together played like a sweet violin in my mind.

"On one very special evening, the energy of our souls interwoven left an indelible imprint irremovable from the universe. All the beauty that I had come to know and that will now live with me forever haunts me with the presence of that special evening and lingers as if we were both ghosts in the room. A part of me left with him, and I could no longer be complete without him. Everything was different: the way the sun brilliantly rose over the hill, saying hello, the way the clothes flapped on the line as if they were in rhythm to music, the branches of the trees moving in harmony with the earth. I felt like I had been blind before Charles entered my life, and now, I was finally alive. I had been reborn. Love had touched me. Love had saved me. Love is the greatest gift of all, Sophie." Rolling her head to the side, Lila stopped for a moment. "I have been truly blessed," she said with conviction.

"We've both been blessed." I smiled softly, wiping the tears from her cheek.

"Sophie, I don't know what's going to happen to me, but if I don't—"

"Stop, Lila!" I said, cutting her words off at the mouth. "Don't talk like that. Don't even think like that. Everything's going to be okay."

"I want to finish my story. I want you to know that love is truth. It is of God."

"I know, Lila." I urged her on. "Go ahead, finish your story."

"Sunday had regretfully arrived, like a grenade in a bouquet of flowers, and as I drove to church, I thought many times about turning Old Blue around. Yet a voice in my head wouldn't allow me to give up so easily. The closer I got to church, the more the anxiety dissipated with the thought of seeing Charles again. I wanted to hear his voice, as it moved my spirit and energized my soul. A creature of habit, I tried to inconspicuously take my usual seat up front, but some members of the church intervened by offering their sincere expression of delight that I was finally well enough to return. I was never good at not telling the truth. Not only did my mind reject lying, my body gave me away, as every surface of my skin would become warm and fiery red in color with any untruth I spoke. However, in this case, it worked well for me because they thought I was still a little under the weather. I may have fooled them, but I didn't fool myself, and I didn't feel good about lying.

"The church began to fill, and I sat eagerly looking for Charles to come out and greet the congregation as he did every Sunday. The choir members were silent, and members of the congregation were patient as everyone awaited his arrival. The delay was definitely out of the ordinary as the service always started precisely at 10:00 a.m. Charles's wife, Vivian, was sitting in the front pew sporting a very expensive hat, exquisitely cut and trimmed with lace that matched her dress and gloves. As I looked at her, I was overcome with guilt and sadness that I had broken their sanctity of marriage, but even more so, that I had broken Charles's vow to God.

"I knew something was wrong, and I began to feel it with every part of my existence, yet all I could do was sit with my stomach turning inside out. With each breath I took, I began to feel more and more constricted as my thoughts drifted into worry and fear. I was sure at this point I was going to hell for having an affair, but I should have started packing yesterday because I didn't just have an affair, I had an affair with my preacher."

"Holy cow! He was the preacher?" I blurted, forgetting to keep my voice down. "Oh my God."

Lila glared at me. "Didn't you want to hear the truth?" she asked humorlessly.

"Hell, yes! This is far better than anything you could make up."

Lila smiled at that, and we both became a little less serious. Even as the night's cold air had settled upon every part of my body, I felt the warmth of her soul, and nothing else existed in this moment except the two of us and the secret that she had been holding.

Lila got back to her story. "A young man who I had never laid eyes on before took the pulpit, and the service began. The service was not at all usual that day. To the contrary, it was quite boring, and for me to confess that, it had to really be boring. Charles had a passion for his ministry, and when he spoke he wasn't just a preacher, he was a true messenger. The word of God was ingrained in every part of his soul, and at times, it felt as if he were speaking for God himself. On several occasions during Sunday services, the entire congregation was so engaged and inspired, the spirit of the Lord felt as present as you sitting right beside me, Sophie.

"I desperately hoped that I wasn't the reason for his absence. The last thing I wanted was to be responsible for taking something so precious away from not only Charles, but the community of fellowship as well. Could he not face me? Were his feelings for me not true altogether? God wouldn't play such a trick on me. Had I played a trick on myself? I most certainly was a sinner and deserved whatever was to come. I had confessed to God many times in my life my illusions of love, what I thought love was, but this was different: no tricks, no illusion. As real as if God himself were standing in front of me, I knew it was real. Two souls, two bodies couldn't have come together as we did on that Saturday evening if it wasn't real.

"After the service commenced, I slipped out and quickly drove back to the farm. Every inch of every mile was excruciating as I thought of Charles and what could have possibly kept him from performing the service. I didn't know what the rest of the day would bring, but one thing I knew for sure was that I had to find a way to get in touch with Charles or I wouldn't be able to sleep another night.

"I hurried up to the house, hoping to change out of my church clothes when I noticed a box on the front porch with a large red ribbon tied neatly around it. Of course, I opened the box quickly. Inside was a smaller wrapped box, as well as a dozen white lilies. I opened the smaller box, and inside was a beautiful necklace, the same necklace I let you wear tonight. There was a note attached that simply read, *Meet me at the pond. Charles.*

"My excitement was uncontainable. I couldn't get to my room fast enough to change clothes in anticipation of seeing Charles again. The air was brisk with a beautiful start to the morning, but due south, the clouds were becoming thicker, and the possibility of a storm was increasing with the warmer air coming in from the south.

"Upon reaching the pond, I saw Charles sitting up against a large log from an old oak tree that had fallen last winter. He appeared deep in thought as he looked over the pond. In the midst of all that had happened in the last few months, it was the first time that he truly looked as if he were at peace with himself. He looked happy.

"Upon hearing me approach, he quickly turned. Seeing me, he jumped to his feet and ran to me. He pressed his body fiercely against mine, and we kissed. No words were spoken. The only exchange was our breath as he gently laid me down on the grass. Our bodies fit perfectly together, and his lips upon mine were exact. I fell perfectly into his arms and body as he did into mine. Lifting my dress, he ran his warm hands up my thigh. I wanted him inside of me, and I invited him eagerly as he pulled my panties down toward my ankles. Unzipping his pants, he thrust into my body with his lips gently pressed against mine. He made incredible love to me. Soon, the thunder began to roll, lightning struck, and our orgasm was as intense as the storm."

Lila's words were compelling and far more honest than I ever thought I would hear come out of a grandmother's mouth. But I respected her for trusting me with the most intimate details of her love with Charles. She was beginning to shiver, so I held her closer. When she seemed ready to continue, I asked, "Why didn't Charles preach at the service?"

"Oh." She laughed. "All that worry was for nothing. He concocted a story about being out of town on business so he could spend the entire day with me on Sunday. Normally, this kind of behavior was out of character for both of us, but I have to admit, I would have done anything just to be with him.

"Through the remaining spring and summer, the pond became our special place where we took respite from the rest of the world. We shared our deepest secrets, talked about our dreams, and thanked God for bringing us together and providing the awe of his beauty and wonder in the nature that surrounded us. It was our playground of love. We shared every possible waking moment together. When we weren't together, I felt as if my breath had been taken away, and in my mind, I reveled in every moment we shared together. Nothing could replace his touch or his breath upon my neck. Fortunately for us, Vivian rarely noticed Charles's absence. Private club meetings, spa treatments, and community events kept her busy climbing the social ladder.

"I found great pleasure in preparing the food for our picnics, and I loved to watch Charles indulge himself and to hear the sounds of enjoyment as he sunk his teeth into a decadent piece of chocolate caramel cake, which was his favorite. Every moment seemed like a celebration of our lives, and we cheered and toasted each other as the glasses of wine chimed together. We laughed and drank until the moon fell upon us and our naked bodies lay peacefully under the midnight sky.

"My guilt was incredible, but it was never overcome by my insatiable appetite for him. Neither of us knew where this was leading. We weren't looking ahead; it was all too beautiful just living in the moment. I felt like a woman again, and I was changing with each passing day.

"Charles loved me with a passion that I had never known before and will never know again. It was the first time in my life that I felt I was truly making love with someone, and I loved him with all my mind, body, and soul. This was a wonderful time, and every memory is ingrained in my mind. I have replayed them thousands of times since that summer, and they still seem as real as if it were only yesterday. Don't misunderstand me, Sophie. I loved your grandpa dearly, and he was a good man, but I was in love with Charles. I hope one day, you will come to understand the difference."

A long time had passed since Lila and I had heard the shatter of the window. I wanted to remove myself for some investigating, but Lila's story kept me firmly seated as she continued.

"Charles was beautifully romantic." She smiled, thinking of him. "Every morning, he would wake before the dawn and pour his heart into words as he wrote tender and poetic letters touching my spirit and moving the very core of my soul. It felt like Christmas every day as I anticipated that wonderful gift waiting to be opened. He made me feel young again, and memories reappeared of what it was like to be a child and experience the sheer excitement of expectation.

"It became a daily habit, after all the animals were fed and watered, to take my morning walk down the old dirt road to retrieve his letter. I would open the letter right away and read each word carefully upon returning to the porch. With each letter, I fell deeper and deeper in love with him. I saved every one and still keep them in a special box upstairs in my bedroom. I take them out quite often to read them over and over again. They kept me alive. I want you to have them," Lila said tenderly, giving the impression that she was passing on her greatest treasure.

I was honored that she was entrusting me with something so intimate and close to her heart. However, I firmly assured her we would be getting off this porch, and she would be reading the letters herself for many years to come.

She smiled that infamous half smile, and taking my hand in hers, she placed both of our hands over her heart. It was then that I realized we had rescued each other—not just from the assault to our bodies, but from a past that kept us captive by our own self-inflicted sentence of guilt and shame.

We rested quietly for a while as Lila's eyes were becoming heavy and her voice weakened.

In a little while, she was able to continue. "It had been a magical summer for both Charles and me. As it was coming to an end, we were both becoming irresponsible in our voracious need to be with one another, even somewhat reckless and cavalier. Oblivious to anything but our own needs, we were unaware that Vivian had become suspicious of Charles's excessive absence at home, as well as his lack of attention to her, though strangely, the latter had never bothered her before.

"One morning, the sun had just begun to rise, and I jumped from the warmth of my bed onto the cold oak floors as usual. Shivering as I dressed, I threw on an extra sweater and ran out of the house, splashing into a cold front of air. I beat the old sun before it had a chance to warm the land. I walked with a spring in my step down the dirt road with every expectation of finding a letter, but to my surprise, there was nothing there. Charles had never missed a day of writing to me, so right away, I knew something had happened. I tried to dismiss all of the undesirable thoughts running through my mind. However, my sixth sense was working overtime, and I felt certain that what I was feeling was far stronger than what I was thinking...and it wasn't good.

"Breakfast was very lonely without a letter from Charles to keep me company. It wasn't until that morning that I realized how much his words on paper filled the void of his absence. The first glimpse of a life without him scared the hell out of me. My fear was short-lived, at least for the moment, when a knock at the door threw my worries to the wind. I jumped from the kitchen table, elated at the expectation of greeting Charles at the door. Nothing could have prepared me for the evil that waited on the other side. It was Vivian.

"I was speechless.

"Standing before me was a statuesque woman with coal-black hair and piercing dark eyes to match. Her fair skin, thin face, and long, pointed nose reminded me of a witch. She stood on the porch and looked at me as if I were a disease she was trying to avoid. Charles had spoken of her only when I had asked about her, and he grieved for the years lost to a woman whose intent seemed to be to destroy anything that brought joy to his heart, no matter what the cost. Hilly often referred to her as the Black Widow, and if you couldn't get along with Hilly, well, you just about couldn't get along with anyone.

"I hadn't prepared myself for this moment. You would have thought that nerves would have gotten the best of me, yet I was as calm as could be. I felt sad for her as she stood holding the letter from the mailbox that Charles had written to me. Though Charles was unaware of it, Vivian had followed him straight to my mailbox, where she had retrieved the letter.

"I had to wonder what a man like Charles would see in a woman like Vivian. They were two polar opposites. One loved life, and the other loved money. One gave his life to serving God, and the other gave her life to serving herself. Charles described her as cunning and vicious. As a young man who was held in high esteem in the community, he had dreams of becoming a minister. When Vivian told him she was pregnant, he did exactly what any honorable man would do in the same situation: he quickly married her, only to later find it had all been a lie. She had tricked him. Devastated and heartbroken from her deception, he took his oath of marriage seriously and chose to remain within the sanctity of his vow, a mistake he said he would live a lifetime regretting.

"Charles dedicated his time to seminary as well as to managing a large farm inherited from Vivian's family, while she spent most of her time away from home, strengthening her social influence. Later during the marriage, they had two sons, Christopher and Jonathon, whom Charles described as the very souls who saved his life. He raised them on the farm. Close in age, the boys became inseparable from each other and from their father. Christopher was in the same class as your mother, and I couldn't believe how handsome and respectful he was. Motherly instinct wasn't something Vivian was born with, and as the boys grew older, so did her jealousy of their relationship with Charles. Soon, she began to ignore them, essentially becoming absent from their lives.

"As she stood before me, she looked like everything Charles had described, something that could be summed up in one word: cold.

"Holding the letter in front of me, Vivian said sternly, 'I believe this is yours.'

"I reached out to take it from her, but she quickly withdrew it.

"'I'll keep this...just in case,' she said, patting the envelope against her hand with a self-righteous smile.

"'Just in case of what?' I asked. Nothing had prepared me for what was coming.

"'I'm sure you love my husband, Mrs. Randolph,' she said arrogantly. 'He's a kind man, but he's weak. Frankly, I'm glad that he's had some companionship lately. I've been busy with my own little affair, but I won't be humiliated in this town, and it's time for this picnic to end.'

"'You don't love Charles,' I said sadly but forthrightly.

"'You're right. I don't. But the last thing I'm going to do is give him up to a tramp like you. I wouldn't be so humiliated. I have a reputation to uphold. It took me years to get to the top, and don't think that I'm going to let it all go because of a meaningless summer fling.'

"I stood silent as I listened to evil spewing from this woman's mouth. I had been in her presence for a mere few minutes, and I felt as if I were dancing with the devil. I couldn't imagine how Charles had survived all those years. She had a vicious tongue that accompanied an empty heart.

"'Don't you want your own happiness?' I asked.

"'You really are as dumb as I thought. Happiness is something that you buy.' She laughed sarcastically.

"'I won't let him go,' I replied staunchly. 'That will have to be his choice.'

"'I'm not giving him a choice,' she replied coldly.

"'And why is that?'

"'Because I can destroy him, and once I destroy him, you will be next. You don't get it yet, do you? I own half of Saint Paul and most of Morton Falls. Charles didn't have a pot to piss in when we met. Everything we have started with my daddy's money. Daddy needed a strong man to run the farm, and I needed a man who was easy on the eyes. You know he still makes love to me whenever I demand it.' She smiled as if she had just stuck her hand in my chest and proudly pulled my heart out.

"'You are vicious!' I stated angrily.

"'Thank you!'

"I was as near as I had ever come in my life to harming someone. I could feel myself losing control with every word she spoke. She had no idea how close she came to being kicked off her high heels and having her ass smeared all over the front porch. 'Get off my porch!' I demanded.

"'I don't play games, Mrs. Randolph. Everyone will know of this affair, including Charles's sons, and I will ruin you. Can you imagine what people would think of you having an affair with a respected minister? He would be stricken from the pulpit for good, the one thing he loves more than anything. I would suggest that you don't mention this visit to my husband. I would suggest that you think long and hard about even seeing my husband again.'

"Enveloped by her chilling presence, I stood frozen, unable to move. As she drove away, my heart fell from my chest onto this very porch. How could I leave Charles in the hands of a woman who loved the designer purse she was carrying more than she loved him, while I loved him more than I loved myself?

"Hour after hour went by as I sat on the porch. Late into the evening, I realized there was only one thing I could do: I had to let him go. I couldn't be the reason for his removal from his church or for his being separated from his sons. I had felt love in the way that God intended it to be, and I had no regrets. My only regret was that I would have to lie to Charles and end the purest love I had ever known.

"Before retiring to bed, I went to the barns to shut off lights, and in the driveway, I noticed the envelope that Vivian had taken from my mailbox. It must have fallen from her purse as she got into her car. She would never have left it intentionally, as she had stated clearly that she would use it against Charles.

"I opened the letter. As near as I can recall, this is what it said: 'Dear Lila, you are the best thing that has ever happened to me. You're my love and my best friend. Every day that goes by, it seems like I discover something new about you to love. It's incredible to me how one person can make such a big difference in my life. You touch me in a way no one else ever has and give me so many special reasons to smile. I've never been so happy. I've never been so much in love. Your love for me and how you show me that love is a miracle. You are an amazing and beautiful woman, and I thank God daily for you and your presence in my life. Forever has new meaning as we walk each day together. Love has new meaning as I now understand what true and deep love really is. You are the woman of my dreams and the love of my life. I'm yours forever. Charles.'

"With each word I read, I loved him more. I knew what she could do to him. I had no choice. I had to let him go."

Lila bowed her head in sadness, and tears fell in remembrance of a morning long ago.

Chapter 19

Lila and I fell asleep for a short time. When we woke, she was even more determined to continue with her story. I wanted her to go on, but my heart didn't know how much more it could handle, and I wasn't sure how much more Lila's body—beaten, bruised, and bleeding—could take. Blood had soaked her pajama gown and now ran along the floor of the porch. I couldn't believe that she was still alive. My body was sore, but I had survived beatings far worse than this from Gabe, and I knew I would be okay. On the other hand, Lila was getting weaker by the minute, and she needed medical attention as soon as possible.

"I'm okay," Lila said, seeing the look on my face. "I want you to know how the story ends. It would be the last time I saw Charles's old pickup drive up the long dirt road to the farm. I can still see him smiling with excitement as he pulled up to the house, and the trail of dust that followed him seemed to disappear as quickly as the words that I had rehearsed. God had certainly created him in his likeness and sent him to me with a smile that brought with it the warmth of the day's sun. As he stepped out of his truck and upon this very porch, I knew this was the last time I could ever hold him in my arms or run my hands across his powerful body. That thought left me numb.

"When I opened the porch door, I stood before him a new woman, a woman created by the blessing of his love, pure and divine. He had given me the courage to open my eyes and see all the beauty that surrounded me. He had given me the hope to believe that anything was possible. He was the reason my heart fluttered like butterfly wings in the sky. He gave me the wisdom and the strength to stand before him today and love unselfishly. He was the very breath of my life.

"The words didn't come easily, but I told him it would be the last time we would see each other. Of course, he begged to know why. He pleaded with me, promising he would leave Vivian right away. He said he wanted to marry me. He said he couldn't live without me. We both cried as I lovingly held his hands and asked him to go back to his family. I told him I loved him, but it wasn't our time. I'm sure he didn't believe a word I said, but if there was one thing I was sure of, Charles loved me enough to honor my decision.

"Dropping to the porch on his knees as if I had stolen his very last breath, he lowered his head in confusion.

"When I saw the look on his face, I couldn't believe what I had done. I wanted so badly to tell him the truth, but my will to protect him was far stronger. Numb, I turned away and walked into the house, leaving him on the porch where our first meeting had taken place, where he had kindly offered me his help. His words played over and over in my mind, and I heard the softness in his voice, the sincerity of his heart. He was an inspirational man of God, and I had just left him kneeling all alone on the porch. I couldn't bear to watch him leave. After that day I became a ghost, a shadow moving upon the earth, a memory that would eventually fade with the passing of each season.

"I retreated to the house for many weeks, taking occasional walks to the pond. Nature had a mysterious way of healing my soul. The wind whispered it would be okay as it glided gently around my neck. The rays of the sun spilled upon my face, bringing with it the warmth of the heavens. The branches of the trees cradled me and moved gently with the wind, rocking to the rhythm of the earth.

"Daily tasks seemed impossible. Without motivation, every chore took twice as long to complete, and the days, once too short, now seemed as if they would never pass. I chose to not answer the phone, and the mere thought of walking to the end of the driveway to get the mail seemed utterly painful. I needed time to suffer and time to heal.

"Robert and Hilly visited frequently, and I managed to convince them that I had a cold I couldn't shake. Although somewhat suspicious, Hilly was a real friend. True to her character, she was lovingly annoying in her attempt to help me, whether by baking something for me or by giving me a rundown on her mother's tried and true medicinal recipes. I appreciated her concern, but what I really needed was peace.

"With the passing of summer and fall soon upon us, I knew I would eventually have to face the music. Hilly was beginning to think I had a life-threatening illness and was about to initiate an intervention. Robert was a true gentleman. He knew indeed that something was wrong, but he allowed God's hand to do the healing. He seemed to speak without actually speaking and loved me without smothering.

"From the time Charles left my porch, there wasn't a day that I didn't think about what he was going through. I knew for every pain I suffered, he suffered with me.

"Every evening, I lay awake in the bed where Charles and I had made love. I would take a deep breath and take in the scent of the pillow where he had laid his head. I held on to the pillow as if I was holding him, and every detail of his body in mine consumed my mind and comforted me as I drifted off to sleep. I thought at some point I would run out of tears, but they were endless, accompanying every painful yet beautiful memory.

"Then early one morning, I was standing on the porch watching the sunrise, and a brisk fresh breeze rolled past me reminding me that a new season was forthcoming. Summer was ending, and fall was moving in. The breeze brought with it a profound message:

I needed to change. I was moving into a new season of my life, a rebirth. Like the strong oak trees that had survived hundreds of years, waking to welcome every beautiful rise of the sun, closing the evening with the glow of the moon, and witnessing all the in-between, I, too, would survive. We are as much a part of nature as nature itself.

"I had neglected a lot of things on the farm the past several weeks, and I desperately needed to get the crops out of the field. It was time to put on my best face, dust the sand off my feet, and put my best foot forward in an attempt to climb out of my sorrow and find peace in my soul.

"Work on the farm kept my mind occupied, taking care of the many things that needed tending to, and with the passing of time, each day became a little easier than the one before. It was about then that I found Hunner near the pond. He was a wonderful surprise, and we began to develop our friendship. He followed behind my every step while I did chores. The list of those chores was never ending. Fences were in need of repair, chicken coop doors needed replacing, and the shrieking sound of the swinging doors in the kitchen was enough to drive anyone mad.

"It was time to get things back to normal, or at least as close to normal as they could be under the circumstances. I had been absent from church for quite some time, and I wanted nothing more than to stay home on the farm, where I felt secure. But I knew I couldn't. It was all part of getting back to normal.

"Church wasn't a place I needed to go to make peace with the Lord. I had already done that in my heart. God stood nearby watching my tears fall into the pond. He sat at my kitchen table while I ate, so I didn't have to be alone. He blew with the breeze into my bedroom window in the evening, and with a brush across my cheek, wished me a peaceful goodnight. I didn't need to go to church to find him. He was living around me, for me, and within me. I needed to go to church to see Charles. As a man, he fascinated me. As a lover, he hypnotized me. As a pastor, he inspired me. It wasn't going to be easy. In fact, I wasn't sure how I was going to react. But I knew it was time. I had to know he was okay.

"Sunday arrived like an unwelcome visitor, and I opened the morning with a prayer. I asked God to give me strength, courage, and the grace to hold my head high and summoned extra backup from Saint Michael to shield and protect me from the arrows of harsh judgment awaiting me.

"I made it a point to arrive early, hoping to take my seat without being noticed. I wanted to elude questions about why I had been gone so long. Unfortunately for me, it appeared to be a morning on which everyone had come early. I once felt so at home there, but now, I felt uncomfortable. I walked nervously toward the front of the church where I usually sat. I was surprised to be greeted with wonderful smiles and warm welcomes from everyone in the congregation, everyone except Vivian and her two sidekicks, Lou Lou Bell and Beatrice.

"I smiled kindly at them anyway. It was a good thing I had summoned Saint Michael's protection. I needed all the help I could get, knowing full well the evil that was before me. I hadn't believed for a minute that Vivian would confess her husband's affair to anyone, including Lou Lou Bell and Beatrice. In order for her to save face, I thought, she would surely keep it a secret. Nonetheless, she had great influence over many people, and whatever it was she told Lou Lou Bell and Beatrice, I realized it wasn't good. The way they blatantly turned their heads not to notice me and rolled their eyes rudely, it was obvious that they knew something.

"Sophie," Lila said gently, "I knew you were curious about why they treated me so harshly, and I believed you had a right to know. I just wanted to tell you the truth in its entirety, when we were both ready for it. One day, karma will come collecting. Unfortunately for these ladies, they will have a big debt to pay, and karma doesn't accept cash or credit cards." We both chuckled, and

Lila continued. "I took my seat in the pew, and the anticipation of seeing Charles caused sweat to surface on my forehead and my cheeks to blush as roses. I could feel how hot they were.

"Suddenly, a young man I had never seen before stepped up to the pulpit and welcomed the congregation with polite words and a charming smile. The entire congregation began clapping, and Vivian quickly stood up to announce that after the service, a welcome luncheon would be held in honor of the new pastor. She continued to tell everyone how excited she and Charles were to have Pastor Evan as a part of the Presbyterian family, even bragging that she had personally handpicked him herself.

"Her smile was as phony as the words she spoke. She kept making eye contact with me as she smiled and told of her intent to spend more time with Charles and her family. I knew many of the women at church envied her life. They saw a woman who had everything: beauty, a wonderful husband, status, and more money than anyone could ever spend. But what was missing from all of this was the truth, and its absence was profound in her case.

"As you can imagine, the hour-long service felt like an eternity. My mind created every horrible scenario of what could have happened to Charles. I had often wondered how far Vivian would go to keep us apart after she had learned of our affair, and I imagined her threatening to expose him if he didn't step down from his duties as pastor. The possibilities were endless, and my imagination ran away with me, my thoughts chasing one another in and out of my mind.

"I'm sure the new pastor did a fine job, but I didn't hear a word he said. After the service, once I was out of Vivian's sight, I politely excused myself from the welcome luncheon and hurried to the truck. I drove back to the farm and fought any idea of trying to find Charles, though I wanted to hear from his own mouth what could possibly have removed him from the one thing he loved most in his life. He had told me he loved being a pastor, that it was his calling, even his first love.

"Did he leave because of me? Maybe it didn't have anything to do with Vivian at all. Whatever the reason, I was perplexed, especially since Hilly hadn't told me anything about a new pastor, and everyone knew she spread news faster than any news reporter or television station." Lila laughed. "That evening, I invited Robert and Hilly over for a cold glass of lemonade and conversation on the porch, at which time I nonchalantly brought up how surprised I was to see a new pastor that morning at church. I knew my invitation was devious, but I couldn't go on another day not knowing what had happened to Charles.

"Hilly acted surprised, as if she couldn't believe she had forgotten to tell me the heartbreaking story. Almost whispering, as if she were delivering a top-secret message and someone other than the three of us would hear, she leaned toward me and spoke three words that left me speechless: 'Vivian has cancer.'

"Hilly sat back in her chair and began rattling on about how she had heard from the ladies at her quilting club that Charles was so devastated that he retired from his position as pastor to spend more time with Vivian. She continued on, but I didn't hear much more. It was as if her mouth was moving, but she made no sound. I had lost Charles forever. I knew he was an honorable man, and although I had his heart, Vivian had the warmth of his body and the kindness of his soul comforting her. I questioned which one of us had the better deal.

"I continued to go to church, and the new pastor was a fine young man, but I missed the enthusiasm and inspiration Charles brought to God's word. He was a tough act to follow. I prayed for Charles, and surprisingly, I prayed for Vivian, too.

"Cancer certainly hadn't softened Vivian or lessened her appetite for destruction. In fact, she seemed even more bitter and ungrateful as the community tried to embrace her with compassion. She was still extremely put out in my presence, and her attempts to snub me were obvious, but I learned to ignore her rude behavior. I found compassion in my heart that I didn't know existed as I prayed for her to find peace with herself and others before she left this world.

"I also had to accept responsibility and admit that I had contributed to her actions toward me. They certainly weren't unfounded. Forgiveness is a hard thing to do sometimes, Sophie, whether it's forgiving yourself or someone else, but it is essential for peace. If Jesus can forgive us for our sins, we should certainly be able to forgive others. Your heart cannot be pure in his love if you are holding resentment for any of his children." Lila spoke sadly as she continued talking of Charles. "I missed him with every part of my being. There were times when I begged God to take the ache in my heart away.

"One evening before the sun set, I was looking out my bedroom window and saw Charles sitting by himself near the pond. I wanted nothing more than to run to him. I grasped the curtain and held on, as if it could hold me back. I watched him intently and memorized this picture in my mind. He was sitting on the old oak log where we used to have lunch and where we lay down in the moist grass to make love. As I watched him, I wondered what he was thinking. I hoped one day he could forgive me for hurting him so. I hoped someday he would understand.

"The winter months were long and harder than any winter I had ever experienced before. Years passed, and there were many times I thought about telling Charles the truth, but all I could imagine was the pain and destruction Vivian would bring to him and his sons. Her cancer, which had originally been identified in the breast, was successfully treated. She remained in remission for many years, but about a year ago, she learned that the cancer had spread to other parts of her body. The day we were shopping for prom dresses, I thought it was unusual that she wasn't shopping with Lou Lou Bell and Beatrice. Although I didn't bring it to your attention, something inside of me knew that her absence had to do with her health. I learned later from Hilly that she was slowly losing her battle with cancer and was becoming more and more frail. She was a fierce woman, and I thought to myself that if anyone could give cancer a good fight, it would certainly be her.

"I decided I could never tell Charles the truth. It wouldn't make a difference now anyway. But I could see his face everywhere. I felt him every time the wind rushed across my body. I woke with him on my mind, and I fell asleep with him in my heart.

"Love isn't something you look for, Sophie. It finds you. It's a miracle sent from God, the most incredible gift of all. It was humbling to know that God loved me so very much that he blessed me with a man he made just for me and me for him. Life is made up of miracles and moments...

"My pain was slowly changing to a knowing, a knowing that although only for a short time, God had loved me enough to let me touch a love so powerful it would sustain me for the rest of my life. I have lived every day since then with love in my heart, for both Charles and God. Although they aren't visibly present, they're both beside me, and that's where I found my peace.

"Sophie, we have many lessons to learn in life, and one of those is that God gave his only son so that we may live. I hadn't been living for many years, how selfish and wasteful of me. But he sent Charles to me, and in a moment, I was awakened. Life had a whole new meaning.

"We're supposed to live, really live, to notice all the beauty around us and to feel all our emotions—not to hide them away and let them eat us alive, but to recognize them, feel them, and then go on living. The only thing we can possess and hold on to is love. Love is never on condition. It is given freely and should be held sacred in our hearts.

"We spend a lifetime searching for love because we create our own illusion of what it is supposed to look and feel like. Our mistake is that we cannot create or control love. It's a miracle waiting to happen to us, and when that time comes, it's real, it's magical, and it's a gift. Love changes us. Who we are or who we believed we were isn't the same anymore. What we are to become is an incredible being who has been touched by the one thing God has asked us to bestow upon ourselves and others, the one and only thing that really matters in this world: love. As love is given freely by God, it comes without warning, at times when we least expect it, and not always at the most opportune time.

"I've waited so long to share this story with someone, and I'm honored to be sharing it with you," Lila said. "I hope you never have to hold on to a secret that long. I love you, Sophie." She drifted off to sleep.

"I love you, too, Grandma," I whispered.

Lila's secret had kept her a prisoner of the truth. It had claimed her heart, and inside, she knew that her only freedom was to surrender all that kept her soul under arrest and to encapsulate her spirit with truth. She faced the fear she had chosen to deny, and she was finally released from the imprisonment of her own soul. The chains had been removed from both of our hearts.

Chapter 20

With the sun peeking over the bright red barn and onto the porch, Rosco the rooster began to crow, welcoming us to the start of the day. The early morning hours had been very cold, and Lila faded in and out as her breathing became increasingly labored. Her body was weak and sore, and the floor of the porch had not been forgiving. I wrapped her tightly with my dress and snuggled her closely in my arms, hoping my body heat would help to warm her. Time had completely gotten away from us while Lila shared her story, and what originally started out on the porch feeling like minutes turning into hours became hours turning into minutes.

I was worried about Blake and Hunner, and not knowing if they were injured—or worse—was agonizing. With no sign of either of them, I prayed, calling upon God to protect them and bring them safely back to me. Time was running out, and I needed to get off this porch and get help soon.

Slowly, I lifted Lila's head from my lap and moved from underneath her. Even with the slightest shift, her face exhibited every bit of her excruciating pain, and I felt helpless to alleviate it. I studied her as she lay on the porch. The warm rays of the sun revealed her beauty and the peace she held within, despite the pain. Although swollen and bruised, her face radiated God's presence, and I believed I was truly in the company of an angel. Lila wasn't a hypocrite like those old church hags. She walked the walk, talked the talk, and was truthful to herself and God. That, I'm sure, was where her grace came from.

Suddenly, the wind carried a sound from the distance. Sitting tall, I looked over the porch wall, hoping to see something that matched what I was hearing. I was sure the sound was that of a vehicle, possibly a tractor, and with any luck, it was headed in our direction. For the first time since arriving on the porch, I had hope. The sound was nearing, and as my excitement escalated, so did my fear. If I could hear something, so could Gabe.

"Grandma, wake up!" I said frantically, carefully shaking her shoulders. Her eyes barely opened, but I knew she was still with me. "I hear something. Can you hear it?"

I raised myself and peered over the porch wall again, hoping that help was on its way. An unfamiliar truck coming up the drive toward the house was traveling faster than our usual company. Fear presented itself again, immobilizing the excitement I felt just moments ago. Could it be someone coming for Gabe? I didn't think I had ever seen this truck before, and the closer it came to the house, the more certain I was of that. Lowering myself from the porch wall, I sat quietly, hoping not to be seen by the driver.

Dear Lord, I pleaded from my heart, *please let this be someone to help Lila.*

Panic began to set in, and I found myself once again shaking uncontrollably as fear took me hostage.

"Sophie," I heard Lila whisper for me. I slid toward her, and she reached out her hand to me. "It's going to be okay," she said. "Remember, we're made from the same cloth. We're survivors." She squeezed my hand.

Her words were encouraging, and she was right: we were survivors.

The truck came to a complete stop in front of the house. A door slammed, and footsteps made their way to the front porch.

"Someone's here," I whispered in Lila's ear.

Her demeanor was calm as she held my hand. I, however, was anything but calm. I feared if I lost her, I would lose myself again, and this time, I knew I could never recover.

Loud, heavy knocks on the front door accompanied a male voice calling for Lila. With no response from within, he continued knocking louder, each time sending my heart racing. Whoever this was, he was completely oblivious to the danger he was arousing on the other side of the door. After a few minutes, the knocking finally stopped and the footsteps began again, coming nearer to where Lila and I lay. From around the corner, a man I had never seen before appeared. He was a tall, older man with graying hair, and he walked with a slight limp. Like most of the farmers in the area, his skin had been roughened and cracked from the harsh sun of summer and the severe cold of Nebraska winters.

I remained silent as he walked near. When he came into full view, Lila lifted her head from the porch and smiled upon the man as if she had seen an angel. "Charles!" she said gratefully. A sigh of relief escaped her, and her eyes closed as she slipped into unconsciousness.

Dropping by her side, he placed his hands gently on her face. "Hold on, Lila," he pleaded lovingly. "Stay with me. I'm going to get help." Turning toward me, he asked, "Who did this to you?"

"I did, old man!" An all too familiar voice echoed from the distance. At the end of the porch, the nightmare was standing, awake. It was Gabe.

"Gabe!" I shouted. "Please don't hurt them. I'm the one you came for. I'll leave with you. Please don't hurt her anymore, please!"

"Shut up!" he yelled. He seemed sober, yet he appeared confused.

"Gabe, please listen to me," I pleaded. "Do you remember when your mother died? You held her in your arms and watched her take her last breath of life."

His eyes became glassy and teared up at the mention of his mother.

"You told me it changed you and that you died with her," I said. "I've been there, too, when I lost my mother. But I've been given another chance, and so can you. Lila needs help. Please let us get her to the hospital."

"No!" he shouted.

"We can help you, young man." Charles was much like Lila had described. He spoke sincerely, and his voice was tender and kind.

Although our lives were in jeopardy, looking at Charles, I felt safe. I no longer feared Gabe. What I feared most was that if I didn't make it off this porch, I would never be able to experience the love that Charles and Lila shared together. I would go to any length to survive. "Gabe, he's right," I insisted. "We can help you. I will help you. But right now, we have to get my grandmother to the hospital. She's going to die!"

"You think you can fool me?" Gabe asked angrily. "I don't need your help, and I don't want your sympathy." His rage grew. "You think you're pretty clever, don't you? You think you can pull at the ol' heart strings, talking about my mother." He laughed to himself as if he were a fat cat who had already eaten the bird.

"I'm not trying to fool you, Gabe. I love you. I've always loved you. Let's just leave. Let's get out of here and forget that any of this ever happened. I promise, I'll never come back." I spoke as convincingly as I could. Lifting myself to my feet, I stumbled a bit in an attempt to regain my balance. Extending my arms, I reached toward him and slowly took a few steps forward.

Gabe's expression changed with each moment. He appeared disoriented, looking about the porch and continually checking over his shoulder, acting as if someone were behind him, watching him. He ran his hands through his hair and rubbed his forehead, and I could sense he was feeling unsettled. Gabe had always been a little paranoid, but the way he was behaving, you would have thought he had seen a ghost.

"Stay back," Charles said, summoning me to come back. "You don't need to get yourself hurt."

"I'm okay," I mouthed at Charles. I continued until I was a few feet from Gabe.

"You're a brave little girl," Gabe said in an eerily disturbing voice.

"I don't belong here," I said, reaching out to touch his hand. "I never did. I'm nothing like these people. You know who I am. Take me away from here."

"You betrayed me," he said angrily. "You know what happens to people who betray me. You're nothing but a whore." He spat in my face.

I wiped my cheek with my skirt. "I did what I had to do to survive here, Gabe. Isn't that what you always taught me—to do what you have to do to survive?" I moved closer to him.

Reaching behind me with one arm, I gripped tightly the sharp piece of pottery that I had tucked in my belt. Fully aware my pleading was in vain, I was ready to fight. Finally, my will was strong enough to save myself and Lila.

"You couldn't survive fighting your way out of a plastic bag," he said, mocking me.

To his surprise, I lunged toward him, and with every bit of force I could summon, I lashed violently at the side of his neck and face. Gabe stumbled backward and crashed into the patio table and chairs, further immobilizing his efforts to retaliate.

Fiercely and with a passion I didn't know I had, I struck him over and over, slicing into his skin as if it were butter. "You were supposed to protect me," I screamed at him. Each time I slashed the broken shard into his skin, I felt as if I were releasing every hurt, every fist he had put to my face, every scar he had left on my body. The feeling, although violent in nature, was invigorating. "You will never hurt me again! You will never hurt me again!" I screamed over and over.

"Stop, Sophie, you're going to kill him!" Charles demanded. He pulled me from atop Gabe. "He's had enough."

Visibly incapacitated, Gabe cowered as he lay twisted among the patio table and chairs. Charles wrapped his arms tightly around me. I fell into his chest and began to cry. I cried a tear for every time I'd ever been hurt, and Charles held on, his arms safely comforting me. I had never felt anything like this before. I realized what I had been missing...a father, a grandfather, a loving man of God.

"Sophie, go inside and call the police," Charles instructed. "Tell them to send an ambulance." He kindly wiped the tears away from my eyes. "I'll keep an eye on this one." He watched Gabe closely. Before I reached the door, he asked in a concerned voice, "Where's Blake?"

"I don't know," I replied with guilt straddling every word. "I think he's hurt, but I haven't seen him since last night."

"Where's my grandson?" Charles shouted. He grabbed Gabe's neck and wrapped his hands tightly around it.

"He's in the cellar," Gabe answered, choking out his words.

"Make that call, Sophie," Charles said with alarm, "and then hurry. Go find Blake."

After contacting the authorities, I made my way as quickly as possible to the cellar. The latch on the cellar door had been locked securely by Gabe. He had used wire fencing from the barn, and it took me several minutes to untwist it. When I got the door open, I saw Blake lying unconscious on the cellar floor. A pool of blood circled the floor around his head. I couldn't tell whether he was alive or dead.

"Oh my God!" I cried. Kneeling beside Blake, I lifted his head into my lap and cried. "Please, Blake, please wake up." I prayed he would.

His eyes slowly began to open. I lowered my head to his and cried in relief that he was alive.

"I'm sorry," he whispered. "I tried to get help. I'm so sorry."

"It's okay. It's not your fault," I said, holding his head close to my heart. "This is all my fault, Blake. I'm the one who's sorry."

"Jealous boyfriend?" Blake asked, rubbing his head.

"There's so much I need to tell you," I confessed.

"Help me get up, Sophie." Blake lifted his head in an attempt to sit up.

"Help is coming. Your grandfather is here. He's on the porch with Lila. Lila's hurt pretty bad. I need to get back to her quickly."

"I'm okay," he said. "Help me get up so I can get some sense about me."

I helped Blake up and stood, holding him firmly. Blood had dried in his hair, but I could see a deep gash where the blood was fresh.

"We need to get you to a doctor," I said, giving him a hand to the stairs.

"I'm okay, Sophie," he replied, in an attempt to diminish my concern. "It's just a little scrape."

Slowly, Blake climbed the stairs out of the cellar. Upon reaching solid ground, he stood for a moment shading his eyes. Coming from the darkness of the cellar, he was nearly blinded by the sun's rays.

I softly placed my hand in his.

Gently, he pulled me closer and whispered into my ear, "I love you, Sophie."

Those words were what I had longed to hear. Blake was more than a girl could ever want. I knew I was going to have to tell him the truth. I could no longer hold on to the secrets of my past. As Lila had opened the box to her secrets, her courage would lead me to open mine. I wanted him to know. I wanted him to speak these words after he knew who I had been and the things I had done.

I reserved a response and replaced it with a smile. "We need to get back to Lila," I said, guiding Blake back to the porch.

From the distance, we could see and hear the police cruisers and ambulance coming up the drive. Swiftly, we walked back to the porch. I wanted to be with Lila at this moment. My heart was heavy for her, and Hunner's continued absence was beginning to bring my worst fears to life.

Approaching the steps of the porch, I thought it amusing to see Charles holding Gabe by the back of the shirt, nearly lifting him off the ground. He looked pathetic. Dangling from Charles's fist, bloodied and weak, he began slurring profanities at Blake and me as we neared. He was certainly no match for the strength of a man of the farm.

Blake directed the paramedics to Lila, while I had a few parting words for Gabe.

Standing a few feet from him, face-to-face, I looked him in the eyes, without fear. "I forgive you," I said, bowing my head. I turned away from him to rid myself of any sorrow, any fear, and any memory that would haunt me again.

"I'll be back for you!" he yelled, spitting at me.

"I'll be ready," I said. I turned to look back at him, then smiled and walked away. I regained myself in that moment. I was Sophie Mae Randolph, and I would never give my power away again.

Dragging Gabe down each step of the porch, Charles greeted the police officers, calling each by name. They handcuffed Gabe and put him into the cruiser.

I looked at him as he sat in the cruiser. He seemed so alone. I thought about the battle he had ahead of him, just as we each have our own battle. Without courage, we remain a victim; it takes guts to be a victor. God gives each of us free will to choose. There are only two roads, and everything lies in our choice. Although it's a difficult lesson to learn and an easy one to deny, we must always consider our choices carefully. No matter how hard or how uncomfortable, we instinctively know the right answer.

The police slammed the doors of the cruiser and sped down the drive. A feeling of peace came over me, and I was free from the past. *Moments like these can't be defined by words,* I thought. *They can only be experienced.*

Paramedics gently helped Lila onto a stretcher and carefully lifted her into the ambulance. I rode by her side to the hospital in Saint Paul, all the while never taking my eyes off her. Charles and Blake followed us to the hospital, and we watched as the paramedics lifted Lila from the ambulance. They rushed her through the hospital doors and into the emergency room.

Blake and I were taken to separate rooms across from one another. Our doors were open, and the beds were situated so that I could see some of what was going on. I could hear some of what was going on as well. A resident intern began to clean and stitch up the large gash in Blake's forehead. Saint Paul's hospital wasn't used to seeing so many people in the emergency room at one time. In fact, with only one doctor on call, I knew I would be waiting for a while. I didn't mind at all. I wanted to make sure Lila and Blake were tended to first and that they were given the best care.

My body was sore, but my spirit was alive and well. I didn't need a doctor anyway. *What I need is a hair appointment,* I thought, laughing to myself.

I saw police officers, accompanied by Charles, head into Blake's room to begin their interview process. They were anxious to put together details of the night that had started with a promise of blossoming love, but ended in tragedy and almost death.

"Can you tell us what happened, son?" the police officer questioned.

"I don't know if I'll be of much help," Blake said matter-of-factly. "I was passed out most of the time. We arrived at Lila's place a little after midnight. When we got out of the truck, right away, Sophie realized something was wrong. We got up to the porch and noticed the flowerpots were broken all over the place. It looked like someone intentionally wanted to destroy everything. We found Lila lying unconscious on the floor near the porch swing. We could tell she was hurt pretty bad, so I told Sophie I was going to call for help. I didn't get very far. I took a few steps into the house, and that's all I remember until Sophie woke me up. When I came to, I was lying cold on the floor of a cellar."

"Do you know who the perpetrator is?" the police officer asked.

"I've never seen him before in my life," Blake replied.

"That's all the questions we have for now, Blake," the officer said. "We hope you get to feeling better."

"Thank you," Charles said, shaking the officer's hand. "You boys do mighty fine work." The officer left the room. I expected him to come my way, but he didn't. Maybe he would after I had been treated.

Sitting in my room, I listened and watched Charles as he lovingly put his arms around Blake.

"I'm glad you're all right, son," Charles said, patting Blake on the shoulder. "You sure found yourself a pretty date." He smiled.

"She's more than just pretty, Grandpa," Blake replied. "She's special."

I smiled to myself hearing what the two had said about me. I lowered my head in thought and drifted away in memories of the night. I felt very alone without Lila, and tears dropped onto my dress and shattered like glass as each fell.

Charles stuck his head in the room and politely asked if he could join me. When I nodded, he sat down in the chair beside my bed and took his hat off, placing it in his lap.

A wave of emotion overpowered any bit of self-control I had left. I felt like I had been drinking tequila all night and been rear-ended by a freight train. I began to experience the same fear of losing Grandma that I had when I lost my mother. A painful cry exploded from my mouth, and I reached out as if to grab Charles's hand for help.

Charles quickly left the chair to sit beside me on the bed. He held me cautiously, and I cradled my head in his chest.

I cried until I was completely exhausted. "I'm so sorry," I said over and over, hoping that God would hear me and bring Lila back to us.

Charles brought his hand to my face and gently caressed my cheeks.

Looking into his eyes, I could see the love that Lila had been missing for so long.

"Sophie," he said kindly, "I couldn't wait for the day to come that I would be able to meet you. Lila spoke of you with such joy in her heart, and I prayed that someday the two of you would be reunited." Charles's voice was deep and affirming and reminded me of the judge who spoke with such compassion. I imagined this must be what a father's voice sounded like.

"You don't understand," I replied, trying to explain. "None of this would have happened if it hadn't been for my stupid letter to Gabe, for my selfishness, my sheer lack of regard for anything other than what I wanted. Lila and Blake could have been killed, and I don't know what's happened to Hunner. How stupid can a person be? What's wrong with me?"

Lifting my chin with his hand and raising my head to meet his eyes, Charles spoke in a commanding voice. "Lila would've given her last breath just to have one moment with you or even a mere glimpse of your face. No matter what happens, you have to understand that her life became full the minute she saw you. You'll waste your time and energy feeling sorry for the mistakes you've made, and there's nothing you can do now that would change anything anyway. You see, Sophie, sometimes the greatest moments are those that are learned in times of tragedy. When fear has ravaged our soul, denying us the ability to act on our own and forcing us to reach to the heavens as if we were clinging to the very last thread of hope, we pray for help. Suddenly, fear no longer exists as he reaches back."

"I can see why she loves you," I said softly, lowering my head back into his chest.

Charles sat quietly with me and held me close to him as we waited to hear news of Lila.

I thought about everything Lila had told me. Her story certifiably had to be the greatest but saddest love story I had ever heard. Though I was shocked to learn that she had an affair, not to mention an affair with her minister, in a weird way, I felt it made her more human. When I thought she was perfect, she didn't seem real to me. When I realized she wasn't, I fully recognized the difference between one person's perception and the truth. Lila always said truth lies in the honor and integrity of the soul, which cannot be seen—only witnessed.

When I first saw her waiting at the end of the hallway in the courthouse, I thought to myself, *What the hell is God thinking, sending me off to live with a holier-than-thou Bible-thumping, Jesus-loving old woman?* It was like mixing vinegar with honey. He certainly had a sense of humor. Months had passed on the farm as I watched her in all her grace, never complaining and moving through each day as if she had the world sitting in her hands. She often walked to the pond by herself and sat alone with her thoughts. All that time I thought she was sad, but looking back, I realized she was anything but sad. To the contrary, the memory of that special place kept Charles close to her heart, and she was full with his love. It finally occurred to me that the picture on the fireplace mantle was that of her and Charles sitting on the log by the pond. It was only now that I could truly understand the significance of her treasures.

"She still loves you, you know," I blurted out. I pulled away from his embrace, hoping to engage him in conversation about Lila.

"I wish that were true," he said, his voice no longer commanding. He lowered his head, appearing to have lost all faith. "I would have done anything to be with Lila." He massaged his forehead with his hands.

"Do you still love her?" I asked carefully, hoping he wouldn't take offense at my nosiness. It appeared our conversation was uncomfortable for him.

Charles hesitated for a few moments. He looked surprised that I would ask such a question. Luckily, he didn't take offense. "You're a very straightforward young lady. In fact, you remind me of Lila," he said. He chuckled, but then turned serious. "I've loved only one woman in my lifetime, and the memory of that love has and will sustain me for a lifetime."

"That's funny," I replied. "That's almost exactly what Lila said. I mean, that your love had sustained her through all these years." For a moment, I thought about what I had just said and what he had just said, and I hoped he meant Lila when he referred to loving only one woman in his lifetime. I hoped and prayed that someday I would come to know a love like that. I was certain I was on the right track with Blake.

Charles looked curious, as if he wondered how much information Lila had shared with me regarding their relationship.

I didn't want to blow the whistle on Lila for kissing and telling, but I wanted Charles to know how much Lila still loved him. "I'm sorry that your wife isn't doing well," I stated, acknowledging my concern for him.

"Thank you, Sophie," he replied gracefully. "That's very kind of you." His face and the tone of his voice were a clear giveaway that his concern for Lila was far greater than his concern for Vivian.

"I hope she makes amends with God, you know, just in case something happens," I said. I was referring to her willfully keeping Lila and Charles apart, though I didn't say so.

Perplexed, Charles asked me to clarify my statement.

I became conscious that Lila had never told Charles the truth about why she ended their relationship. Realizing that I had just opened a huge can of worms, I had nowhere else to go but down, so I thought I might as well spill the beans.

I told Charles every detail of Lila's story as we sat together on the hospital bed. He listened, sometimes smiling and sometimes in anger and disbelief. He finally knew the pain that Lila had been living with since he had been gone and the absolute love she felt for him, so real, so truthful, and so strong that she would do anything, even if it meant letting him go, to protect him from any harm. Her undying love for him was without condition. We sat quietly, joined in love by a person who not only touched our hearts; she touched the very being of our souls.

Blake walked into my room with a large bandage on his head covering the stitches. He stuck his chest out as if he were about to crow, exhibiting a cockiness I hadn't seen before, but one I liked anyway. "I'll bet nobody can beat our date!" he joked.

Charles and I laughed. I couldn't wait to give Blake a hug. He kissed me on the cheek, and Charles looked at both of us as if he were looking into a mirror of his heart.

Blake reached out to Charles and, shaking his hand and patting him on the shoulder, thanked him for helping. "You're lucky you didn't get yourself killed, Grandpa!"

"Tough as nails, son. Tough as nails. Look at these guns," he said jokingly as he flexed his arms.

We all laughed, and I realized the testosterone in the room was at record levels. I was in fear of growing a mustache, or something like that.

Moments later, the doctor came in and reported that Lila was doing well and we could see her. I jumped excitedly from the bed, but soon recognized that my body wasn't moving as quickly as my will to see Lila. The doctor refused to let me out of the room without checking my condition. Charles and Blake waited in the hall while he did a brief but thorough examination. He confirmed what I already knew: I would be sore for a few days, but nothing appeared broken. He also agreed a hair appointment would be needed.

Entering Lila's room quietly, Charles took his hat off and went to her bedside. Blake and I stood silently by the door, witnessing the reunion of their souls. I prayed that nothing would ever separate them again.

"You saved me," she said kindly, reaching for Charles's hand and smiling her famous half smile.

Leaning over and kissing her on the forehead, he softly whispered back. "You saved me."

Blake and I left them alone and retreated to the waiting room, where we met with the doctor. Lila was going to be okay, he informed us. She just needed a few days of rest, and he would be keeping her in the hospital to monitor her. There were no internal injuries or broken bones. She was one tough cookie. We were two of a kind. Her strength in God carried her, and my strength in her carried me.

I stayed at the hospital with Charles and Blake into the evening. Lila asked to speak to me alone before I went back to the farm. Sitting beside her bed, I listened.

"Sophie, I have something to tell you. I'm sorry I didn't tell you last night." She spoke sorrowfully, and her voice, still weak, trembled. "But I didn't know how to tell you then, and I don't know how to tell you now." She paused. "Last night, shortly after you and Blake left for the dance, a young man came to the door. I hesitated to answer because when I looked through the screen door, my first thought was that he might be a drifter. He wreaked of alcohol, and covered with tattoos, his appearance wasn't very inviting. He noticed my hesitation, but spoke politely, telling me he was a friend of yours.

"I opened the door slowly and told him you weren't going to be home for the evening, but he was welcome to come back tomorrow. I don't think that's what he wanted to hear because in an instant, his expression changed, and it became very obvious to me I was in danger. I tried to pull the screen door shut, hoping to lock him out. But faster than you could blink an eye, he was through the door and began attacking me." Lila hesitated for a moment and took a deep breath before continuing. "I was about to pass out as the man held his hands around my neck, when suddenly Hunner lunged at him and took hold of his arm with his teeth. I yelled for Hunner to release him, but naturally, Hunner would die protecting me. Fierce and powerful, he fought relentlessly, holding the young man at bay for several minutes. Hunner managed to pull him down on the floor, and by this time, he had inflicted quite a bit of damage to the young man. I honestly thought that Hunner was going to kill him.

"Then in an instant, Hunner fell over and lay gasping for air on the floor. I ran to him and lifted his head, pulling him close to me as he took his last breath. I told him how proud I was of him and that he would always be my hero.

"The young man left little time for me to grieve and began kicking me. In my favor, however, his strength had been significantly diminished by the hurt Hunner put on him. My rage and strength, on the other hand, significantly increased knowing what he had done to Hunner. We fought for several minutes, but he eventually overpowered me and knocked me unconscious. When I woke up on the porch, I began praying for you."

Careful not to hurt Lila, I crawled up on the bed and lay beside her. We cried together and remembered Hunner.

"I know how much you loved him," she said quietly, wiping the tears from my cheeks.

My heart couldn't survive much more. The loss of my mother had been unbearable, and the mere thought of losing Lila took me to my knees. How was I to cope with losing Hunner? He had been my best friend since I arrived on the farm, and we loved each other almost from the first moment we laid eyes on each other. Her words tore through me like a knife ripping my heart out. I thought of the way he followed one step behind me everywhere I went and the way he looked at me with his deep brown eyes as if he knew my every thought. I couldn't bring myself to believe that he was gone, and I couldn't bear the thought of never seeing him again.

I was so ashamed for what I had done, for the pain I had caused for so many. I wanted to die. The guilt alone was insufferable.

Chapter 21

Upon arriving back at the farm, Charles and Blake dug a grave for Hunner by Grandpa's garden, and that Sunday evening as the sun fell, we laid him to rest. I patted down the last shovel of dirt, and Charles, being the eloquent messenger of God that he was, recited the most beautiful prayer I had ever heard. Blake made a wooden cross from some old barn wood and painted the name *Hunner* on one arm of the cross. On the other, he painted the word *Hero.*

After our short burial service, Charles retreated to the house for a glass of tea, leaving Blake and me alone for a while. We found a nice patch of grass by Hunner's grave and sat down to rest.

"I'm so sorry for everything," I said honestly.

"I want you to promise me something," Blake said.

"Okay," I replied cautiously.

"I'd really like it if you would stop saying you're sorry." He smiled, but he was serious.

"I'll try." I smiled shyly.

Blake reached over to kiss me, but before our lips met, I leaned in to whisper in his ear, "I love you."

We kissed and sat silently, taking in the freshness of the air and reveling in each other's spirit.

Before leaving, Charles asked Blake to wait in the truck for him, as he wanted a few minutes alone with me. "Sophie, I've been keeping a little secret of my own," he confessed.

I listened intently, knowing that whatever Charles had to share, it was important.

"I left the little puppy by the pond. It was a gift to Lila. I wasn't sure if she wanted him, but I knew she would need him, and I made sure she would find him. I placed him in the tall grass by the pond where we used to meet, and I watched from a distance."

"Why didn't you fight for her?" I questioned. "She really didn't mean what she said. She always loved you."

"I know that now, Sophie. And I knew it then. Even though she acted as though she wasn't in love with me anymore, I knew something else was pulling her away. The kind of love we had, it's not the kind that ever ends. Whatever reason she had for ending our time together, I knew I had to honor it, knowing full well she had to be doing it out of love."

"Thank you," I said gratefully. I kissed Charles on the cheek.

Charles and Blake left, and I sat alone with Hunner and my thoughts late into the evening. I relived over and over in my mind the memories of my life. I tried to remember as far back as I could. I saw Mom and me at the park as she swung me through the air. I saw the merry-go-round that always made me so dizzy. All of the good times, the good memories, had resurfaced and had slowly replaced the bad ones that I had let consume me... let consume my life. *Why is it that in a clear blue sky full of white clouds, we sometimes tend to hold on to the black clouds the most?* I asked myself. That's what I had done since losing Mom. I held the dark clouds as if they were the foundation of my whole life, and all along it had been my choice.

It wasn't until the date of my court hearing and I met Lila that my life changed. From that day on, my heart had been healing, and I had learned to look at the white clouds in the sky. Nothing in this world could ever take that away. I caught my mother's smile in the breeze as it passed the farm, and I held it in my heart. As Lila said, "We are always going to have bumps in the road. Go over them, but don't get stuck on them. Just keep going down the road."

When I first met Lila, I believed she was my curse, but with the passing of time and her graceful teaching, she slowly became my savior. I'm not sure what she saw in me, but there must have been something. In her lessons, she taught me that it is with selfishness that we look for others' weaknesses, but with compassion we search for their strengths. She loved deeper than many will ever come to know.

A few days later, Lila was released from the hospital, and after getting her home and settled in, I went outside. Evening was upon us, and I wanted to sit with Hunner for a while. I lay back on the cool ground and stared into the sky. The stars seemed so close, almost as if I could reach out and pick them out of the sky.

I was so deep in thought, I hardly noticed Lila as she came out to join me. Her body still very sore, she clumsily tried to lie back on the ground. Once she was completely on her back, she took my hand, and we looked at each other and all of our memories, everything we had known, everything that we had learned, all that we had shared. Our eyes teared up, and without saying anything at all, we knew each other as if we had lived each other's lives. We both took a deep breath, knowing that we weren't stuck on the bump anymore; we were going down the road. Where that was going to lead us, we didn't know, but we had each other and a new sense of love and life.

"We should go inside," she said. "Chores on the farm are behind, and we have a lot of fences to mend tomorrow."

As we walked to the porch, I thought about the many fences that I had had to mend. I laughed to myself. "Couldn't we clean out the chicken coop or something like that?"

Lila laughed out loud, and we went inside together.

Chapter 22

Spring arrived, and Blake and I were preparing to graduate. I would still be required to complete summer school, and I was okay with that because Blake promised to meet me at the pond every day after class to fish. We wore ourselves out talking, laughing, and fighting over who caught the biggest fish. Blake and I shared our graduation parties at the farm, with Lila and Blake's mother putting together the biggest spread of food that I've seen, enough to feed the entire towns of Morton Falls and Saint Paul. Charles kept picking food off the table, and Lila kept slapping his hand lovingly. When she wasn't looking, he would grab another cookie.

Eventually, I shared my truth with Blake. I had put myself through hell, holding on to the belief that I was damaged goods and not worthy of loving. My fears were unwarranted, as he accepted me with compassion and love.

Vivian passed away only a few weeks after Lila was released from the hospital. Lila and Charles picked up exactly where they had left off. The only thing that had come between them was time. Watching the two of them together was refreshing as a cool rain on a hot summer evening, and if I wanted to know what real true love looked like, all I had to do was look at them. They wore their love upon the smiles of their faces and upon their hands that touched everyone they loved. The ray of God's love emanated from their souls, encapsulating and hypnotizing anyone in their presence. That is as close as I could come to explaining in words the truth in love.

Lila and Charles saved their wedding until the fall. They both loved all the colors of God's golden palette. They were married right beside the old oak log at the pond. I loved to watch them together. He always touched her so softly, and she looked into his eyes as if she were looking into her own soul. They kissed often, held hands, and you wouldn't find one without the other. They had truly been blessed with God's love.

The wedding was even more beautiful than anyone could ever have imagined. Lila wore a Bohemian-style floor-length dress. Handmade rosebuds attached to a delicate bead necklace gave the ivory silk taffeta gown a naturally attractive style. She wore a soft chiffon shawl, and she let her hair flow, placing pins throughout as she had done with mine for the prom. She looked stunning.

As Lila and Charles stood by the old oak log, leaves in every color of fall fell from the standing oak and showered their ceremony. Nature was in perfect harmony, and God had created a spectacular day for their ceremony. Their vows were nontraditional, and each had prepared a melody of words in order to sing their love for one another. A small reception was held at the farm afterward with family and friends from both Morton Falls and Saint Paul. It didn't include the church ladies.

Charles and Lila's life together was full. Charles eventually turned the management of both farms over to his sons, and he spent almost every waking moment with Lila. He helped her to realize her dream of opening her own bakery. She laughed and told everyone that he was the taste tester at the bakery. He proudly carried that title, and it also began to show on his belly.

Blake and I left for college that fall. As the years passed by, the farm was always close to my heart, and I visited quite often. Blake was my great love, and Lila always said I was blessed to have found him so young. She had waited many years for Charles.

We married shortly after college, and our first daughter was born five years later. We named her Lilly Mae. She inherited the traits of the family: blue eyes and locks of blond curls that cradled her shoulders. Lila said she was the spittin' image of me.

Blake got his degree in engineering, and I got mine in journalism. I wanted to make sure that one day I could put together the greatest story of life's lessons and love on paper. We had our occasional bumps in the road, but we never got stuck; we just kept going. I loved to take Lilly to the farm. Lila would tell her stories as they sat on the old swing on the porch, and Lilly would listen intently. I liked to watch them together, another generation of tough cookies bonding on the porch.

I spent many years wondering if I should try to reconnect with my biological father. After a lot of soul searching, I finally made a decision to leave the past just that—in the past. I had the love of so many, and my life had become so full. I couldn't believe that I ever once doubted the love of God.

Cancer slowly ravaged Charles's body, and he died in the spring of 2012. Grandma lay down beside him as he took his last breath. She laid her arms across his chest and held on as if she wished she could go with him. She laid her head on his shoulder, and with a handkerchief to her face, she cried softly. Lila's will to live after Charles left diminished. She was ill with a broken heart and died only months later in the fall. We carried out her burial wishes and scattered both her and Charles's ashes at the pond where they had played together, where they had joined their bodies and their souls. It was their sanctuary.

So it is on this cool day in the fall that I come back to the farm to take care of Lila's belongings. Stepping up onto the porch, I believe it squeaks louder now than the old screen porch door. Never in my dreams would I have believed when I first walked up those steps leading to the porch that they would be the very steps that I long to stand on now. Isn't it only wood and chipped paint? Hardly. This porch has a story, a life. It breathes with truth and love. Time has left the imprint of our lives here forever. Every memory is fresh in my mind. Every word that Lila shared, her love, remains in my heart forever. I slowly enter and walk through each room, reliving scenes of our lives together. As I enter her bedroom, I feel as if I am in some way invading a place that Lila held private in her heart. A box on the nightstand beside her bed is labeled with my name. I sit down in Grandma's rocker and slowly open the box.

There is a note for me, a message.

Dear Sophie,

All the while you were healing on the farm, in your search for peace, I found mine. One cannot find peace without teaching it. You saved me!

All my love,

Lila

P.S. On top of my dresser, I've left you an envelope. You will find the necklace you wore to the prom with Blake. I found it while cleaning the porch, and I knew, one day, I would pass it on to you. It's very special to me. Charles gave it to me on my birthday, and I treasured it with all my heart. I have also left for you the letters I received from Charles. I give you permission to share our love. It brings with it many gifts, and these gifts cannot be kept for ourselves alone, but rather must be shared with others if we are to know them as our own. My daily walk to the mailbox was with the greatest anticipation, and every word he wrote was a beautiful testimony of his love. I have been truly blessed!

Letters from Charles to Lila

My dear love,

Each day that I get to spend with you is such an incredible gift. You are truly the woman of my dreams, and I love you so deeply and so eternally. I appreciate your kindness, your love, and your special way of talking and laughing with me. You make me whole. You complete me. I want to spend the rest of my time on this earth loving you and showing you how much I love you. I wish for you a truly wonderful and productive day...close to me.

Eternally yours in love,

Charles.

My dear love, my one and only love,

How precious it is to find that one person on the face of this earth that you were meant to be with, for this lifetime and beyond. Thank you for all you do and for your patience with me, always teaching me and showing me the way of love. I do love you so much and appreciate your love and beauty. Each day with you is an incredible gift that I cherish. Thank you for showing me the way and for loving me all the while.

> Forever yours in love and joy,
>
> Charles

My dear love,

Yesterday as we fell asleep by the pond, I lay next to you, and as you were falling asleep, I was telling you that I love you. I continued to tell you and to let the angels know that you are my everything. I know that I'm so blessed and that we're blessed and have been given so much. Know that I love you so much, and I'm thankful for each day that you are in my life. You make all the difference.

> Forever in love, yours,
>
> Charles

My dear love,

It is with extreme comfort, peace, and joy that I write this love note to you this morning. I'm so deeply grateful for your love, patience, kindness, and caring of me, even when I get grouchy. Sometimes, I just laugh and reflect on us and our interactions. You teach me so much in every way. You are my rock and my salvation. You are my everything.

> With all my love,
>
> Charles

My dear love,

Thank you so much for your kind and loving attention last night. I realize that a bath and a leg rub at 3:00 a.m. were not what you had in mind for last night. (They weren't what I had in mind, either!) You always show such love and compassion to everyone, and I really admire that about you.

All my love forever,

Charles

My dear love,

Just a note to thank you for the love, patience, and devotion you show me in all ways, always. I had a beautiful weekend with you and cherish every moment that we have together. May God bless you. We have shared so many treasured moments filled with love, understanding, and romance that make me so thankful to God for bringing us together. You are always in my thoughts and forever in my heart.

All my love,

Charles

My dear love,

I just wanted you to know that you are the love of my life. I've waited for you...and searched for you...for what has seemed like forever. But now we're together, and that is real and cannot be threatened. I love you more than anything in this world, and I'm looking forward to spending forever and eternity with you. Being with you feels so good that I find myself missing you even before we say good-bye.

Forever in love,

Charles

My dearest love,

I can't tell you how comforting it is to be so much in love with my best friend, and to know that we'll be together forever, loving each other. Today marks day 37. I look forward to each day even more than the last. It's hard to believe that my love could grow with each passing day, but it does. I love you so deeply, with all my heart and soul. I will always be there loving you, holding you, and caring for you. You are all I've ever wanted in my life, and I'm so very grateful to God, the angels, and the universe for you and our very special love.

All my love forever yours,

Charles

My dearest love,

Each day, I grow more and more fond of our time together, more focused on our future, and deeper in love with you. My world is so different than it was just two short months ago, and it is all because of you. I hope that I show you and tell you each day just how much I love you and how much you mean to me. Your love is a home for my heart, and when you smile, my heart melts all over again. I love you now and forever.

All my love forever yours,

Charles.

Sue Ann Sellon
Author's Bio

Sue Ann Sellon was born and raised along the Missouri River in Nebraska City, Nebraska, home of the internationally celebrated Arbor Day. Married to her husband and best friend, Dr. Paul Sellon, together they share a love and interest in their historical home and a taste for cooking. Sue Ann was previously a chef and owned her own restaurant, as well as, a fashion franchise. Sue Ann has four grown children and six grandchildren.

Secrets of the Porch, an inspirational romance is Sue Ann's second novel. Her first novel, *Carly's Calling* was released in 2003. Sue Ann hopes to write many more stories that speak to the power of faith and the endurance of the human spirit.